They Never Came Back

Kira Parke

Published by Kira Parke, 2020.

This is a work of fiction. Similarities to real people, places, or events are entirely coincidental.

THEY NEVER CAME BACK

First edition. October 17, 2020.

Copyright © 2020 Kira Parke.

ISBN: 979-8227605849

Written by Kira Parke.

Table of Contents

Chapter One...1

Chapter Two...9

Chapter Three 16

Chapter Four 23

Chapter Five 30

Chapter Six 37

Chapter Seven 44

Chapter Eight 51

Chapter Nine.. 59

Epilogue... 66

Chapter One

People call me a lot of things. Bitch. Slut. Witch. Or worse. To some I'm a complication; a fly in the ointment; a real pubic hair on the motel soap. To others, I'm more than that—a threat and one that should promptly disappear by any means necessary. A friend of mine calls people in my line of work: Hidden Hands. We're the gun under the table. The gun you don't see 'til it's too late. To a few—those who've reached a point in their life where shade has snuffed out the light—I am not only a last resort, I am a Seraphim sent from the heavens. I don't know about that. My name is Zady Proya and I have a complex relationship with all things godly. If I'm honest, I prefer being called a witch.

Let me tell you a story. Let's start at a little King's Cross coffee house. It was filled with the usual brand of transients, try-hards, and has-beens. You know the types. I tried to convince myself that I wasn't one of them as I necked a handful of aspirin with my paint-stripper-strength long black. It hit me in the guts like a bowling ball. The bearded barista who had made the concoction had irritating please-like-me-eyes. He watched me from across the café and I pretended not to notice. It was hard: I notice everything. I noticed the two women talking in hushed tones at the table opposite. They were most likely breaking up, judging by their body language. I'm good at deciphering body language. I noticed the balding man trying to discreetly look down the top of the waitress who was dutifully cracking pepper over his eggs benedict. I also noticed that his wife was noticing it too.

A thin man in his mid-forties made a big show of reading a leatherbound book of poetry. Lord Byron. Wanker. His expensive collared shirt was the color of phlegm. His woolen trousers: a kind of shitty brown. His closely shaven face had the sheen of moisturizer and his eyes had an odd, pulled look—like he'd just recently gone under the knife. I wondered if this was his first mid-life crisis, or just one episode of a whole series. His woody aftershave filled the room and frankly, made me feel the subtlest tinge of nausea.

I massaged my temples before tying back my dark hair with an elastic band. My gray eyes felt as though they might pop out of my skull at any moment. Do you like how I casually throw in the odd descriptor, so you can picture what I look like? That's how I roll. Anyway, I caught my reflection in the polished surface of a metal napkin dispenser—my normally caramel-colored skin had paled to a hue not unlike bald-pervy-man's hollandaise. Not good. I stood up a little too quickly and the room began to pirouette like a drunken ballerina. Please-like-me-eyes lurched forward from behind the coffee counter, making a show of how he might just run to my side—check if I was alright or something. He didn't.

I smoothed out my burnt orange blouse, careful to ensure my hands lingered over my breasts. Was phlegm-shirt watching? No. I faked a yawn, followed by a mildly orgasmic grunt. Yes. I had him now. I casually 'dropped' my bill so I could bend over to pick it up. My dark blue stretch jeans did their job and phlegm-shirt was hooked. I grabbed my brown leather bag off the seat opposite and threw it over my shoulder revealing a hint of bra-strap.

After paying the bill—being sure to cut please-like-me-eyes off before he could ask me out—I left the café and turned right down Darlinghurst Road. I listened out for phlegm-shirt's footfalls, which proved easy enough as he was wearing hard-soled mules that assaulted the concrete with every step. Prey and predator walked the long line of strip clubs, souvenir stores, and sex shops as the clouds massed and the smell of rain defeated the scent of cheap perfume and pathos. 'Hope this wraps up before the storm comes,' I thought to myself as I turned into the park. It was early afternoon but the thick, dark clouds made it seem like nightfall had come early. 'Good. The darkness is good.' People everywhere began dashing for shelter. Fewer people meant less chance of rubber-necking, which was a real bonus.

I slowed and pretended to search my bag for an umbrella.

"Ahoy there, milady!" called out Phlegm-Shirt.

'Milady?' I thought. 'Fuck me.' I spun around. "You talking to me?" I answered.

"You know I am," he began. "Where is the lovely maiden headed?"

"Home before the rain." I dabbed my bottom lip with my tongue and smiled.

"You don't like getting wet?" Phlegm-Shirt asked.

I stood to my full five-feet-nine and thrust out my chest. "Not really, no. Not 'rain-wet' anyway."

A homeless man lay sprawled on a bench not five meters away. He yelled something out to no one in particular before rolling over and drifting off to sleep.

"You've been coming to The Brewer's Bean for a few days now. I'm in there all the time. Should I be flattered?"

"Do you *feel* flattered?" I asked.

"Maybe. Women in that joint seem to appreciate the more refined, older type," oozed Phlegm-Shirt.

"You get a lotta' action outta' the place, then?" I pushed.

"I do alright. You're a little older than the sort I usually attract."

"I've just turned thirty. How young are we talking here?"

Phlegm-Shirt looked me up and down. "Young," was all he said in reply. "So, where do you hail from?" he asked, his voice dripping with forced gentility.

"Surry Hills."

"No, where are your parents from?"

"Mum's from Jo-Berg." Phlegm-Shirt's eyebrows knitted together. "South Africa," I clarified. "And Dad was from Latvia."

"You're like a Mulato, then?" said phlegm-shirt.

"A what now?"

"Like a half-cast," added Phlegm-Shirt.

"Sure. I guess. Did you start up this conversation to quiz me on my mixed-race situation, or what?"

"Sorry, love. Being a bit rude, aren't I? I'm Gordon." Gordon held out a hand yellowed with cigarette smoke and I moved forward, grabbed it and shook.

"Beyonce. My name's Beyonce."

Phlegm-shirt's expression hardened and his voice lost a hint of its original pretense. "That right? Like the singer? You're bullshitting me."

"No. Wish I was. Dad was a real kidder," I lied.

"I like your kind. Sorta' black—sorta' not. Something dirty about it."

"You like 'dirty', huh?"

"Course I do." Gordon ran a hand down my arm. "So do you."

"Is my addictive personality showing? You're confident. I'll give you that," I said with a grin.

"Why don't we head to your place and I'll show you how confident I am?"

"Not so sure about that, Gordon. Bronson hates it when I bring strange men home."

"Bronson? Bullshit, Beyonce. You're not tied down to one partner. I know your type. You're as down to fuck as I am."

"A real romantic, hey Gordon?"

"Look. Let's cut the act!" Gordon grabbed my arm and jerked me back and forth. The homeless man looked up, mumbled something and stumbled off into the shadows. "You knew what you were doing—shaking that ass all the way down here. You can't just turn me on then turn me off like a light switch, you little cunt!"

That did me. My vision blurred and I felt a jolt surge through my body—from the soles of my feet to my scalp. Time slowed as I brought the heel of my hand up to Gordon's nose, noting the satisfying snapping sound as it broke. He released his grip on me and I delivered a punch to his throat that sent him reeling backward. Gordon threw haphazard fists, easily blocked and countered with a kick to his crotch. When Gordon doubled over in agony, I brought a knee upward, punishing his already ruined face.

The man dropped like a sack of shit. I stomped his genitals as he squealed like a pig. Vomit erupted from his mouth and tears filled his eyes. I brought my booted foot down again and again, until he stopped writhing and just lay there—taking it. Lucky for him, I chose not to pull my knife from its ankle-sheathe. I looked around for witnesses before legging it out of there.

Then came the rain.

THE DOCTOR LOOKED AT me, his eyes lingering on my blood-stained top. He tapped a pen against his gray-trousered knee and squinted. His blazer had seen better days and his salt-and-pepper hair was unkempt. Even his glasses looked slightly greasy. The man needed some good news.

I scanned the office; I loved the life-size plastic skeleton and the break-away ear canals, eye-balls, and other assorted horrors. It was Halloween in this room all year round.

I'd been seeing the same Doctor for a number of years. Our relationship had evolved of late.

"You really messed him up?" the Doctor asked without making eye-contact.

I placed a hand over the Doctor's, causing all pen-tapping to cease. "I'm not naïve enough to suggest that he won't repeat what he did to your daughter, Doctor Li." I squeezed the Doctor's knee. "Hopefully he'll think twice at least."

Doctor Li exhaled and his eyes met mine. "Call me Charles. You've done more for me and my family than you'll ever know." Charles smiled. "Just not Charlie or Chuck. Hate that shit."

"Got it," I replied. "So, about that other thing?"

"I'll write you a prescription. For what you've done for me."

"Just one?"

"There might be a repeat or two. But one day, Zady—"

"Yes, yes," I interjected.

"One day," said Charles emphatically. "One day, I'm going to ask you to rethink some of your choices."

I stood and headed for the door. "Charles. Thank you."

"Thank *you*. I really lost it when that prick got off—on a fucking technicality. What kind of a justice system lets a monster like that walk?" Charles steadied himself, his fingers digging into the armrests of his high-backed leather armchair. "Jenny will never know what you've done for her, with any luck. She's seen enough ugly to last a lifetime. Shit—I'm talking about my seventeen-year-old daughter as though she were middle-aged. She's barely begun her life. I'm happy you made that asshole pay for doing what he did. For using her like—"

"It's okay, Charles." I nodded. "It's okay."

"Don't take too many of those," Charles called out as I disappeared into the waiting room and out onto the street.

I CLOSED MY EYES AS the codeine did its work. My stomach felt like a bathtub filling with warm water and a wave of comfort enveloped my body. It took ten tablets to do the job these days: almost half a box. Oh, for the days when the good stuff could be bought over the counter. Sure, I'd tried other things. Booze was clumsy and cannabis made me feel like I was trying to run through a sea of molasses, but pain killers—pain killers did precisely what they promised. The tablets prescribed by the good Doctor Li were like the Rolls Royce of codeine tabs. Too often, I had to rely on the kind purchased on the street. It was all a bit hit and miss. But when it was good, it was *so* good.

I opened my eyes, enjoying the rain pummeling my loungeroom window. I slumped into my Chesterfield, barely registering the chattering panel of news delivery agents on the TV. Wet snuffling at my bare feet signaled the curiosity of my bulldog: Bronson. Curiosity as to why there was no food in his bowl no doubt.

"How about *you* make *me* dinner, B?" I said, as I dropped a languid hand and scratched the beefy dog on the head. Bronson's tongue flopped about, painting his pushed-up face. "Mama can't afford steak right now, baby. Hell, I can barely afford the rent on this place. Feel like home delivery, fella? A fajita?" The dog mewled softly. "Yeah, you're good for a fajita. Where's my bloody phone?"

Mozart's Requiem rang out through the apartment as though in answer to my question. Dammit. Some prick was calling me and disturbing my me-time. I looked about and finally saw my phone peering back at me from the abandoned handbag still laying crumpled in the hall. I flopped off the couch as Bronson ran for the hills and I began to crawl on all fours to answer the call. I'm normally not so keen to answer the phone verbally; I much prefer text. The codeine must have really been agreeing with me.

"Yello?" I muttered. Who the hell answers the phone with *yello*?

The voice on the other end was female. Older: about forty perhaps. Tortured. "They left. Just for a while, it was. Just going down the coast. Don't worry—we won't do anything stupid. When I didn't hear from them, I was concerned, but—"

"May I ask your name?" I asked, not feeling entirely present.

"Someone put me onto your ad online. The Last Resort, it said. Odd jobs. A friend told me you do more than just *odd jobs*. You do *more*, don't you?"

"We should really meet up. Don't say any else on the phone," I said.

The caller's breathing quickened. "I thought it was just for a little while. They never ... They never came back."

Chapter Two

The woman's eyes were puffy and bloodshot and her breath smelled of expensive gin. I paced up and down the dark wooden floor, stopping to get a look out of the huge window at the water view (also very expensive). The sitting room was as big as my whole apartment. The art on one wall alone would have easily been worth enough to *buy* my bloody apartment five times over. Still, it had an air of neglect about it, and not in a cool shabby chic way. The armchairs were worn and the rugs were littered with wine spots and god knows what else. There was a rotten smell about the place. It came in subtle waves and at first, I thought I'd imagined it. After a little looking about, the culprit lay in full view: a bowl of once wet cat food in a silver bowl under a small rosewood table. Looked like it hadn't been touched in a week. Where was kitty? Probably lost in the immensity of the house.

Dust hung in the air like a cloud of sickness and the lady of the house looked as worse for wear as the halls she haunted. Ironically, the Rose Bay house was proudly named: Darkwood—the tasteful plaque with the mirrored letters that hung outside near the front door said so. It reflected sunlight into my eyes as soon as I rolled up not five minutes earlier, like it was thrusting the home's mildly tarnished status into my face. I hate having things thrust into my face.

I snuck a couple more codeines into my mouth as I pretended to look out at the vista and knocked them back with a slug of sparkly water from the crystal tumbler handed me by the help. I turned and looked at Puffy-Eyes.

"I'm going to be blunt: I'm not normally a missing persons kinda' person," I stated.

Puffy-Eyes looked about the room, as if to say: *do you see money being a problem here? Do it for the money, tiger.* What she actually said was: "Then, why are you here?"

I eyed a framed photo of the family: Puffy, the daughters, and two other men. I nodded like I was acknowledging the answer in my head. "So, let's get this straight, ma'am—" I began.

"Call me Dinah."

"Okay, Dinah. Let me get this straight. Liana and Lisa—your daughters—left for the coast with..." I looked at the scrawl in my small spiral notepad, "... Daniel and Lucas, at around ten in the morning on the sixth?"

"Yes," replied Dinah weakly.
"And how old are your daughters?" I asked.

"Liana is sixteen. Lisa is..." Dinah began to cry again. I ambled over and placed a hand on a pink shoulder pad. I hate when bitches cry. Dinah looked like she was in her late thirties but it was hard to be sure. Her hair was dyed blue-black and her face was about two sizes too small for her skull. Her pert cat's bum mouth was smothered in lip gloss (a little juvenile if you ask me) and she smelled, not of Chanel but of the sickly sweetness often pedaled by young starlets who exit limo's sans underwear. I figured she was the kind of mother who wanted so much to be mistaken for her daughter's sister. Lame.

I thrust a hand into the pocket of my gun-metal-gray trench coat. That's right—I'm *that* kinda' gal. The kind who wears a trench coat. Deal with it. I continued with my questions. "And Daniel and Lucas?"

"Um." Dinah looked up at the coffered ceiling. "There are cobwebs up there! Vanessa!"

The twenty-something year old maid blew in looking more than a little put out. We locked eyes momentarily and her whole beleaguered life unfolded in an instant. "Yes, ma'am?" croaked Vanessa.

"Well? Look up, silly girl!" snapped Dinah.

Vanessa looked up. Her silky raven hair was flawlessly braided and her dark eyes were almond shaped. She had a pronounced overbite but it sort of suited her. She was a little knock-kneed and heavy in the rear but not unappealing. Her skin was like alabaster, so the hickey on her neck stood out like dog's balls. "Pardon me, what am I looking at, ma'am?" she asked with the merest hint of an Eastern-Euro accent I could have spotted a mile off.

"The sodding spider webs!" said Dinah.

"But I don't see—" began Vanessa. I felt my stomach acid rise for the poor girl. I could just make out the sound of the radio playing in the background. The first movement of Vivaldi's Four Seasons was in full swing. I focused on that.

"What did you say?" demanded Dinah.

"Sorry, ma'am. I'll get right onto it."

"Not now! You'll do it when our guest has left!"

"Yes, ma'am." Vanessa disappeared like a good automaton and I made a big deal of finishing my sparkly water.

"Sorry about that. She's been distracted lately. Probably drugs. So help me, if I find out that it IS drugs—" raved Dinah.

"About the boys," I interjected before the tirade could waste any more of my time. "Boyfriends?"

"Oh God, no!" asserted Dinah. "They're just ... friends."

I raised a brow. "Not to put too fine a point on it, but are you sure of that?"

"They're good Christian boys. Daniel's eighteen and Lucas has just had his seventeenth birthday. I bought him a leatherbound bible and a very smart tie. Yves Saint Laurent. For church meetings."

"Church meetings? You attend these church meetings?" I asked.

"Sometimes. I'm very busy. I have social events—fundraisers and such," insisted Dinah. My face must have come over all judgey. "Heard of the All-Mothers, have you?"

"Not as such, no," I replied. Dinah looked hurt.

"Oh. Well, I'm the founder. We help young people who come from less than ideal circumstances. Beaten, abused, or just unfortunate."

"You mean poor?" I asked. 'What would *you* know about being poor?' I thought.

"Yes." Dinah sat up proudly in her raggedy-ass Chippendale chair. "If one can't use one's wealth to look after those beneath their station, then what use is one?"

"Quite," I answered with mock poshness. "Forgive me, do you have a partner? Husband?" I began. "Wife?" I added.

"Husband!" Dinah shot back. "All that carry on with gay marriage. It's not Godly."

"And what does *he* do, if you don't mind me asking."

"Is that relevant? Can you help me with my children or not?" said Dinah, her lip already quivering.

'Christ, not more waterworks,' I thought. "Dinah, I'm going to do my level best," is what I actually said. It was true: I needed the cash. "I just need to get a clear picture of your comings and goings. It helps to give me context."

"You're not a real detective, though," Dinah stated more than asked.

I crouched down beside the woman. "I'm a real human, Dinah. I'm a human that's going to help you. I know it's hard to trust people. Hell, I can count the amount of people I actually trust on one finger." I held up the middle one. Dinah laughed—the kind of laugh that's more a rush of air through the nose. "If you've got someone else to turn to, then go right ahead. But if you're sticking with me, then I'll need you to be open with me. For Liana and Lisa." I was sure to use the kid's names. It had the desired effect.

"Yes. You're right." Dinah adjusted herself. "What do you want to know?"

I TOOK MORE CODEINE on the way home from Dinah's place. The answers about her husband—and other things—weren't so much shocking, as odd. The pills helped me think. I had a lot to think about. I flipped through my notes as I walked to the bus stop—did I tell you I don't have a car? You're asking 'why' and that's fine, but we have other more pressing matters to address first. Moving on. I knew better than to ask why Dinah hadn't called the cops. That was none of my business and, frankly, people relying on the fuzz was detrimental to my line of work.

I'd made a note of the picture I'd seen inside. Dinah finally pointed out her husband; he was tall, broad, and hard to get a read on. The girls were brunettes with upturned noses, freckled skin: cute as buttons. There was a man standing beside hubby: she didn't say who that was. Was there a family resemblance? It wasn't a super sharp pic. I should have pressed a bit harder. I knew I would have to hone my questioning skills if I wanted to diversify my skill set.

It was when I re-read my entry about the mystery phone call Dinah had received the day before—the call that motivated her to reach out to me—I stopped in my tracks. Beefa. I'd have to go and fetch Beefa.

I hailed a ride from my phone and before long I was headed to the mean streets of Newtown, on the city fringe. As the buildings and traffic whizzed by, I wondered what I was getting myself into. I was good at roughing up rapists and sabotaging scumbags; this was a little outside my wheelhouse. I patted my left jacket pocket and felt the satisfying bulge there. The envelope contained at least a grand—enough to keep me in coffee and pain relief for a good while, with the promise of more to come. Who still pays for things with cash-filled envelopes? Dinah did. Perhaps she'd seen it in movies and thought she'd better act her part.

Perhaps she didn't want any discoverable evidence of the whole affair. Affair. Who was the maid boffing? That hickey looked serious. Was Mr. Dinah sucking on the help's bits on the sly? Where was he? Did he even care that his kids were missing?

As we stopped at the traffic lights on Broadway, a girl of no more than twelve years of age smoked a cigarette with a friend of roughly the same vintage. They wore thick makeup and mid-riff tops and skirts that looked more like glorified belts. An older man leered at them as he walked past and another called something out from a passing car. I wanted to wind the window down and tell them to 'straighten up and fly right', or some other claptrap my parents probably said to me when I was their age. Was I really that old now? The pit of my stomach bubbled and I feared for them in that moment. As the car took off again, I felt something like sadness—heavy and insistent—in my gut.

The car pulled up outside Beefa's warehouse abode and I spilled out after handing off a way too generous tip. The driver audibly yelped. I hit the intercom and a pause preceded a crackly buzz. The latch clicked open and I pushed through the heavy door into the cool quiet of Beefa's sanctuary. Incense and candles burned and the low sound of Gregorian chants came at me from wall mounted speakers. The vast open plan of the space was broken up with huge bookshelves and screens—great, thick articles of woodwork smashed together by big calloused hands.

I wandered toward the kitchen island on the far side of the place and knocked on its surface, as though summoning the man I needed so much to see. I opened the fridge door and pulled out a beer. Home brew. I'm not a big drinker but I never could resist Beefa's ale. I helped myself to a slice of air-cured wagyu and a pickle (also homemade). As I munched and sipped, I sauntered past a row of plinths featuring busts of Greek philosophers and Roman gods. I ran a hand over the cool marble of Apollo's forehead and suddenly, the sound of flapping made me look upward.

A cockatoo set down on a wooden rafter and released a loud squawk. "G'Day, Cockrates!" I called out. It's pronounced like Socrates with a 'C', if you're wondering. Beef had an odd sense of humor. That's when I heard it: no more than a quick flash of something, like fabric rustling. I gently placed my beer bottle on a table, looked at the ground and focused on listening for a repeat. Nothing.

"Beefa?" I called out, knowing full well how stupid that was if it wasn't who I was expecting. In our line of work, the odd unexpected guest was par for the course. "It's Z!" No response came. No one called back: 'It's me! An intruder!' Surprise, surprise.

I got down low, scooted up to a sideboard, and took cover. I peered out in the direction of the disturbance and waited. Reaching up over my head, I felt around until my fingers hit a solid-feeling human skull model made of resin. Beefa sure knew how to decorate. I leaned forward on my haunches—weapon in hand—and looked out across the warehouse.

Surprise is an awful thing at the best of times. I hate surprise parties, surprise dinner guests, and don't start me on surprise pregnancies. So, it goes without saying that I was less than impressed with the hands that grabbed my lapels, lifted me up, and threw me across the room. Surprises suck.

Chapter Three

I managed to tuck and roll—hurling the skull at my assailant as I landed in a crouched position. I missed but it must have looked way cool, although I had little time to bask in my own bullshit. My attacker was on me in an instant, throwing hands, feet, and knees in my direction at lightning speed. I blocked what I could and absorbed more than a few strikes to my abdomen. My stomach is hard but it still hurt. I had to mentally detach from my physical feelings; imagining that I was just pure spirit watching what was happening to my body from above. It's a thing—try it some time.

A freight-train-fist came at my face and I deflected it with my forearm, spun, and pulled my ankle-knife. Placing my knee on the brute's barrel-chest, I threw my weight into him, taking him down to the floor. My blade against his throat, he looked straight into my eyes and smiled sardonically. I felt pressure in my ribs and chanced a quick glance: he had a field-knife pressed into me. Checkmate.

"Well done, Beef," I said.

"I'd pay you the same compliment, but I'd be lying," replied Beefa before throwing me off him like I was little more than a stuffed teddy bear.

I hopped up onto my feet. "Screw you, you big lummox, what was wrong with that?"

"Oh nothing. If you don't count the fact that I snuck up on you in the first place. Your senses are dulled, Z." Beefa thrust his knife into a sheathe behind his back. He scratched at his thick, brown beard and raised a bowling ball shoulder; the resulting cracking sound echoed through the warehouse. "You using?" he asked without looking at me.

"No," I answered, putting away my own blade. "Okay, yes, but it's only while my back heals."

Beefa rubbed the back of his crew-cut and then placed his meaty hands on his hips. His army-green t-shirt was bone dry: not a hint of exertion. Show off. He spoke in a slow, deliberate way—like a father to a wayward child. I hated when he did that. "Your back is healed. Has been for months."

"I still have the odd bad day. Anyway, you're getting off topic, since when do you jump me when I visit?" I asked.

"It's a new element I'm incorporating into your training. To keep you sharp." Beefa thrust a hand into the pocket of his black cargo pants and leant against a huge, black angel statue. He produced some sunflower seeds in a snap lock bag and Cockrates wasted no time dropping out of nowhere to eat them. "Can't keep you sharp if you insist on disappearing into a chemical fugue," he drawled in his meaty baritone, balancing the big sulfur-crested bird on his veiny forearm.

I shot him an icy glance. "You're like a tall, muscly dog with a bone. Let it go!" I threw myself down on a worn chaise longue and propped my feet up on an antique coffee table. "Anyhoo, I'm here to bring you in on something."

"A job?" he asked as Cockrates, having hoovered up every offered seed, flew off for the sanctuary of the ceiling. "You haven't asked me for an assist for ages. What's got you spooked?"

"I'll tell you on the way," I replied. "After you feed me."

BEEFA'S TRUCK RUMBLED to life and I fished a map out of the glove box at his bidding. I unfolded the thing, knocking my friend in the face more than once, and sighing loudly for dramatic effect. Bronson whined in the backseat as though he felt my pain.

"Dude. I appreciate the fact that you stopped to pick up my dog. What I don't appreciate is that you will not use GPS," I said from behind the wall of map. "Even your beloved military use GPS."

"No. The harder we are to trace, the better. Anyone tracks your phone, it'll be right where you left it: in the artillery box on the kitchen counter," said Beef as we pulled out onto the main road.

"Where you MADE me leave it," I shot back. "Can't expect much more from a dude who decorates his kitchen with used artillery boxes, though, can I?"

Beefa chuckled dryly. "Nothing wrong with a paper map, Z. Indigenous Australians didn't even need that. Some used songs to navigate the country. Each landmark had a song and traveling groups would sing them and directions to the next one would be revealed in the lyrics."

"Nice use of 'Man-splaining', but still pretty cool." I folded the map in half. "You want me to sing you a song?"

"You want me to crash the truck?"

"Fine, smartass. Your loss."

The urban soon gave way to the suburban and soon we were hurtling down the motorway toward the southern coast. There weren't a lot of cars on the road and I pretended for a moment that I was a teenager again, heading for some beachside caravan park with friends. I didn't have a lot of money but staying near the water made me feel rich somehow. I wondered what Liana and Lisa felt when they traveled this same road not more than a week and a bit earlier. Did they sing together? Sleep the whole way? Were they excited, or were they just getting away from home; from an absent father and a sad, neglectful, but still somehow fussy mother?

"So, you going to deliver your mission brief soon?" asked Beefa as he tore into a strip of beef jerky made by his own hand.

"Oh, you want my intel, soldier?" I said mockingly.

"Affirmative."

"Beef. The client's daughters went 'down the coast', then they went missing."

"How's she know they're missing?" asked Beefa.

"Lisa and Liana. They're fifteen and sixteen respectively and they're responsible kids. Dinah—the client and mother—said they always call when they're away, to confirm their safe arrival. They didn't this time. Then the client received a phone call from someone whose voice she didn't recognize. It really messed her up."

Beefa spoke through a mouthful of dried meat. "And?"

I pulled my notebook from my trench coat pocket. "He quoted a scripture at her. From the book of Romans. *Therefore, God gave them up in the lusts of their hearts to impurity, to the dishonoring of their bodies among themselves, because they exchanged the truth about God for a lie and worshiped and served the creature rather than the Creator...*"

Beefa thought for a moment. "Dishonoring their bodies how? The client have any thoughts on it?"

"No. She's under the impression that they're perfect little cherubs and not teens with swarming hormones," I replied.

"Worshiped and served the creature other than the creator?"

"Yeah. That bit worried me too."

"We could be in over our heads here, Z," stated Beefa. "Hidden Hands can strike at a lone assailant easily enough. You and I could probably handle three, maybe four." He scratched at his beard. "But if this is some Satanic cult situation—"

"Let's hope it's not," I said. "Look, it's just a couple of silly kids off with their boyfriends—no matter what Dinah says—and, who knows, maybe they've run off with some neo-hippy commune."

"Boyfriends," repeated Beefa. "Seems clear cut. But the whole thing makes me feel ... I don't know."

"Yeah, I'm afraid I do," I replied.

WE PULLED INTO THE service station as the sun was just beginning to disappear behind the green hills beyond. I exited the vehicle (least, that's how Beefa would have phrased it) and opened the rear door. Bronson flopped out of the back and took himself off for a quick constitutional. We were only another hour or so away from our destination in Ulladulla and two hours away from the city, but we may as well have been in another world. A man in a checked shirt, with the sleeves apparently ripped off, leered at me through the convenience store window whilst picking his teeth with a credit card. A fifty-year-old woman with bleached hair leant against the female toilet door just opposite the petrol browser we were filling up at. She stared at me unblinkingly for five minutes before telling me to 'get fucked'. Reasonable advice.

Beef finished pumping gas and headed inside to pay. Checked-Shirt spilled out into the cool evening and whistled sharply at me before drifting past Get-Fucked into the shadows behind the servo dumpster. I did a double take before he whistled again. Was he beckoning me like a dog? What was I meant to do—trot after him on hands and knees and suck him off right there next to the garbage?

"Hey!" whisper-shouted Checked-Shirt.

My vision blurred. I marched over with clenched fists and stared the man down. "You whistling at *me*, asshole?" I seethed.

"Calm down, mate. I'm carrying."

"Carrying?" I echoed.

"I've got gear," he said.

"I know what it means," I spat as I made out like I was going to walk away. I didn't. "You got codeine?"

"Mate, I got everything," he answered as I sidled up to him, looking around for prying eyes. "I could tell you were strung. How many you need?"

"Gimme' the ton," I answered.

"A hundee? Come on. Not worth my time for less than two," he oozed.

"I sniffed and massaged a temple. "Fine. How much?"

"Shit-biscuits," said someone behind me in a deep voice. I turned to see Beefa with his arms folded across his chest.

"Don't panic, my man. Your girl here just wants to get nice and chill so she can service your dick later," said Checked-Shirt. I cringed. He should *not* have said that.

Beefa pushed past me, advancing like a bear about to maul a much smaller, more terrified bear. He slid his hands under Checked-Shirt's armpits, picked him up and threw him into the wooden fence behind. Checked-Shirt kicked at the ground and tried to get up, though it sounded like he was having trouble breathing. Beefa crouched down next to him. "I see you peddling this shit again, I'm gonna' twist your head off, do you copy that?"

Checked-Shirt nodded.

I hopped from foot to foot; at once gratified that my best friend in the world was so protective of me, yet frustrated that I didn't get to complete my transaction. "You'd best answer him!" I called out to Checked-Shirt.

"C-Copy," he replied.

"Good answer," replied Beefa before popping Checked-Shirt in the mouth. He didn't move after that. "We're Oscar Mike," yelled Beef over his shoulder at me. Oscar Mike means 'we're leaving', in case you're wondering. I could tell he was mad. The madder he was, the more military jargon he used.

Beef stood up, about faced, and marched back to the truck and I watched him carefully, ensuring his focus was off me for the moment. I snuck over and poked Checked-Shirt to ensure he was out for the count. I also checked his pulse to ensure he wasn't dead—Beefa hits hard. My dealer was fine and I thought it only polite to relieve him of a little extra weight. I tucked the hefty bag of pills into a side pocket, admittedly enjoying the weight of it. I ambled after Beef, doing my best to look like I hadn't just stolen drugs off the unconscious body of a drug peddler.

I whistled for Bronson and he obediently appeared. Our odd little party boarded the truck for the remainder of our voyage into god-knew-what. With the supply of medication I had tucked away, I thought I would be able to weather any storm the fates had lined up for me. I was so very wrong.

Chapter Four

I checked my notes and confirmed the name of the motel the kids had reportedly booked into. *The Come on Inn.* Awful name. The requisite faulty neon sign flickered on and off and the place felt dingy and devoid of hope. It was hardly five star and I wondered why four teens from wealthy families (I guessed that Daniel and Lucas came from money too), would stay somewhere so 'common people'. Maybe they enjoyed the thought of slumming it. Maybe it was an *up-yours* to their respective mummies and daddies. Either way, despite my first impressions, it was beginning to look pretty damn good after the hours spent on the road.

"So, how does this work, Super Sleuth?" Beefa still clutched the steering wheel even though we'd parked. "You head on in to the check-in office and rough up the clerk?"

"I have no frigging idea," I replied as I opened the truck door. After pointing a finger at a fairly put out Bronson, indicating for him to 'stay', I hopped out and crunched gravel to the sliding door. A slender boy, in jeans that hung several inches below his waist, threw his skateboard around like he was swatting at flies. There were no flies. I tried not to stare as I entered the reception area. "Evening," I said to the middle-aged, yet somehow still pimply man behind the counter.

"It is that," he replied dryly before sipping on a bottle of something bright blue. "Aren't you hot?"

"What?" I snapped back.

"In that trench coat," clarified Pimples.

"No," I said in defense of my cool fashion statement. "Just meeting some friends here. Didn't think to make a reservation first. You wouldn't have a couple of rooms available?"

Pimples stared at me and then back down at his laptop. After what felt like ages, he ran his fingers over the keyboard and locked his dewy eyes back onto mine. "Yep. How many nights?" His thick spectacles fogged over and I wondered if the sudden surge in clientele was too much for him.

"One. For now." I leant against the ice-cream fridge near the door and tried to look casual. "Hey ... you couldn't tell me if my friends have checked in yet? Liana, Lisa, and two guys."

"Under what last name?" said Pimples, flicking limp orange hair out of his eyes.

Shit. I'm usually so careful *not* to press for names. Real names. Surnames. Mine is a world of aliases. But in this instance, a bloody family name would have been really helpful, Zady! "Uh, okay, you got me. I'm not their friend. They hit my car on the motorway some time back—did a buttload of damage. I followed them here to confront them, but I chickened out at the last minute. Now I'm back for another go at it—if they're still here," I lied, and pretty bloody expertly too.

Pimples played with the collar of his black Ramones t-shirt. "So, how did you know their first names, then?"

Shit! I leant in so I was nose to nose with the highly underestimated Pimples. "Look. I'm not trying to start a whole thing here." I reached into my coat, felt about for my fat envelope and pulled out a one hundred dollar note. It hurt me in my soul. "We can keep the questions out of it, can't we..."

"...Jayphen," offered Pimples.

I stifled a giggle. "Jayphen. Nice name. Strong. Suits you," I lied once more before handing Jayphen ten percent of my advance. He snapped it up without hesitation. Bastard.

"They checked in over a week ago. You're a bit late if you wanna' catch up with them."

"How's that?"

"They never checked out officially. But they're not there. I can tell you that much," said Jayphen.

"How long have they been gone for? Did they say anything before they upped and disappeared?" I asked.

"Couple days I'd reckon. And I don't make a habit of fraternizing with guests. You could have their room. Maybe," teased the greedy prick. "I left it as-is in case the coppers wanted a look."

"But no coppers have come, have they?" I paused before handing Jayphen another hundred. "Hang on. Room? Singular?"

"Yeah." Jayphen looked up and smiled greasily, revealing a set of very crooked teeth. "Two beds."

"Calm down, tiger. Keys?" I demanded, pulling back and holding out my hand.

"It's a hundred for the night," oozed Jayphen.

I massaged my temple. "You cool with dogs?"

BEEFA THREW HIS BAG on one of the poorly made beds and looked around the room. Bronson retired to the toilet for a drink and I checked each and every drawer, every nook, every cranny. You're probably waiting for me to tell you about how I nearly gave up, that is until I found that last minute, all important clue. The odd thing is: I didn't find a damn thing. There weren't any stray belongings suggesting a good time was had. No abandoned underwear, no condom wrappers, no evidence of teens being teens.

"You sure he gave you the right room key?" asked Beefa before dropping to give himself fifty. He did that often.

"Bloody hope so. I paid that pimply turd a small fortune. It's like ... Like they've been erased."

"Ten, eleven, twelve," huffed Beefa.

"You're right. Maybe they checked in, like good boys and girls, and then cheesed it to some other location so the *real* vacation could begin?" I said in Beef's direction.

"Twenty, twenty-one."

"Why check in here at all? To throw Momma off the scent of course," I replied to the question Beefa hadn't asked.

"Thirty, thirty-one!"

"They didn't check out so peppy little Jayphen out there would have plausible deniability? It's not a great plan but young peeps aren't always great planners. Think I'm onto it, or just blowing hot air?"

"Fifty!" announced Beef as he rose to his combat booted feet.

"Thanks. Good talk," I remarked.

"What?"

"Never mind. This is a dead end, isn't it?" Bronson chose that moment to emerge from the bathroom and shake his dripping wet jowls.

"Yes," replied Beefa matter-of-factly.

"Well, what now?" I asked, staring at the stained ceiling. A knock at the door made me jump. "Hey, thanks!" I said to the ceiling sarcastically.

Beefa—always the take-charge guy—opened the door with a sharp: "Yes?"

"You guys looking for Leese an' them?" said Slender-Skateboard.

"You are?" queried Beef.

"Torrens. I'm Jayphen's brother—your girl met him inside," said Torrens. What possesses parents to name their spawn Jayphen and Torrens?

"Not my girl," corrected Beefa.

"It's hurtful how quick you were to qualify that, Beef," I added, as I sidled up to my not-boyfriend. "You mean you know Lisa?" I asked Torrens.

"Yeah. Her and her friends left real quick the other night. Some guy was looking for them," Torrens said.

"They were scared," said Beefa.

"Why do you say that?" I asked.

"They exfiltrated without a trace." I looked back at Beef quizzically. "Cleaned up like teenagers generally don't."

"I take your point," I said. I turned back to Torrens. "You didn't tell your brother?" I asked.

"Nah. Fuck that guy. He won't gimme' any shifts anymore. Says I got no customer service skills." Torrens rolled a skateboard wheel up and down the door frame. Some trademark red hair poked out from beneath his beanie.

"You just hang out here?" asked Beefa.

"You been down here before, man?" droned Torrens.

"Not recently," answered Beefa.

"There's nothing to do. Nowhere to go."

"So, where would four kids go in a place where there's nowhere to go, if they were running from some guy?" I asked.

"Maybe I know where they went," said Torrens, raising an eyebrow before a heavily pregnant pause.

"And?" I prompted. The lad certainly shared Jayphen's genes. "I'm not paying you, Torrens. Just be thankful my friend here is not in the punching mood."

"Fuck this." Torrens made to walk away but Beefa—god bless him—clapped a huge hand on his arm and threw him into the room before slamming the door shut.

"Speak!" shouted Beef.

"Leese was the hot one. I liked her. So, I told her they should hide out under Burrill Lake Bridge. Me and my mates go there to smoke and fuck around sometimes," babbled Torrens.

"I'm guessing they paid you for such comprehensive local knowledge," I said.

"Yeah," answered Torrens, as though I'd asked the most stupid of questions. "But I asked Leese for a blowjob first. She was too frigid to deliver."

Torrens released a shrill scream and Bronson barked as Beef threw the skinny lad across the room and into the wall. He just loves throwing people into stuff.

I glared at the crumpled idiot on the floor. "We should go. Jayphen would have heard that," I stated. Bending down so that Torrens could hear my voice at low volume, I said, "And *you*, stop using young girls as sex toys. Respect them and a whole world will open up to you. Take the opposite route and someone like me will deliver unto you a whole world of physical pain, you dig?"

Torrens said nothing, so I drew back my fist until he flinched. "Is 'dig' old people talk for *understand*?" he squeaked.

Beef piped up. "Come on. We're—"

"Oscar Mike?" I interrupted.

"Copy that," said Beefa.

OUR SHITTY INFORMANT had failed to point out which end of the expansive bridge he'd suggested as a hideout. After finding nada at the northern end, we headed for the south side. There was a marina and a fair bit of nocturnal activity, so we parked a block away and hoofed it back. Bronson insisted on accompanying us and I didn't object. Our badass trio edged cautiously toward the grassy bank that descended to the bridge's underpass. When we felt it was safe enough, we headed down into the shadows to take a look. It was hard to see anything.

"If I had my phone, we could use its flashlight," I whispered to Beefa.

Beefa silently pulled a torch from the thigh pocket of his cargo pants and flicked it on. After scanning the area, I was convinced that we'd come up short. That is until Beefa tilted his head like he'd heard something I couldn't, broke out into a sprint, deftly climbed the retaining wall, and disappeared behind a pilon. Bronson looked up at me and I shrugged before following after.

I rounded the column and it took a moment for my eyes to adjust. Finally, I saw it: two girls hunched over a boy—a boy laying in the dirt and covered in blood. I fell to my knees and began looking him over.

"Knife wound. Under the left arm. Missed the axillary artery, but it's still pretty bad. Likely to get infected," said Beefa in an unwavering staccato.

I looked at the two teary girls. "Lisa. Liana?" They sobbed. One harder than the other. I grabbed the slightly smaller of the two by the shoulder and shook gently. "Lisa?" I guessed. She nodded.

"H-How do you know who we are?" asked Liana, each word delivered between shuddering breaths. Her dark brown hair was plastered across her freckled face; her jeans were stained crimson but she looked unhurt.

"Your mum sent me. Is this Daniel or Lucas?" I asked.

"D-Daniel," croaked Liana. Daniel mumbled something in response. He was white as a sheet.

Beef grabbed Liana's hand and placed it on Daniel's wound. "Pressure. Here," he said firmly but gently. He looked at me then back at the girls. "Who's got Lucas?"

"Gideon," said Lisa, her voice hard and tinged with something. Rage perhaps.

"Who's this Gideon?" I asked. There was no answer. "Lisa. I'm only here to help. I'm not a cop. I don't want to harm you. We can get Lucas back but you have to give me something."

Lisa's eyes met mine and she slowly lowered her head as though praying to some unseen thing. Her delicate features were soon shrouded by a curtain of dark hair. The sudden change in demeanor chilled me to the bone. "No one's *getting him back*," she said with cold mockery. "Gideon's my uncle. And he's pure fucking evil."

Chapter Five

Another motel: *The Castle of the Coast*. Cute. I took care of the details at the front and quickly met Beefa who carried Daniel into our room with Lisa and Bronson in tow. I hoped against hope that we wouldn't attract any undue attention. We placed Daniel on the bed and I went back to Beefa's truck to fetch his—very well stocked—first aid kit. Beef had driven his truck to our impromptu accommodation and I had to drive Lucas's vehicle, albeit illegally. It was a nice ride—a Lexus. Little Lucas and his fancy-ass Lexus. He was surely still on his L plates, but I didn't see any on the sedan. Either he had just decided to risk it, or Daniel had driven them on their coastal odyssey.

Once I'd retrieved the kit, I sprinted back to the room. Beefa was already examining Daniel's wound. Lisa was standing at the bedside, her arms wrapped around her and that steely expression on her face. Liana was kneeling next to the bedside table. As a churchgoing gal, her form was perfect. I began working on Daniel; Beef cut the boy's t-shirt off and I cleaned up the gash under his arm. The knife-wound was a particularly nasty one. The boy's brown hair had a slight curl to it and it was soaked with sweat. His eyes rolled around in their sockets and he reminded me of nearly every movie I'd seen about demonic possession. They're my guilty pleasure. Don't judge me.

After I was done stitching, I had Liana hold the gauze in place as I began to bandage up the patient. I figured I'd involve her rather than watch her slowly melt into a puddle. If either girl was going to open up to me, it was her. Lisa was an iron fortress—I'd seen enough of her kind to know it on sight. I asked Liana to apply a cold compress to Daniel's forehead and I hoofed it back out with Beefa to grab the teen's luggage from the car. I bid Bronson stay to look after the teens with the promise of meat as his reward. I didn't want the girls hovering around outside if their uncle really was the prick Lisa had said he was.

The bags were stylish, and nothing to call home about, save for one: a black lambskin duffel with the words Saint Laurent emblazoned on the front face. Yves Saint Laurent? Why did that ring a bell? I stopped in the motel carpark, taking cover behind a minivan to avoid any wayward sticky-beaking. I dropped my load in front of a bemused-looking Beefa.

"What's the delay, soldier?" Beefa asked flatly.

I pulled my notepad from my jacket pocket and flicked it open. After scanning it, I smacked the page triumphantly. "Bloody knew it!"

"Explain," said Beef.

"Yves Saint Laurent. I bet this bag belongs to Lucas," I exclaimed.

"How do you know that and why do we care?"

"Dinah said she'd bought Lucas a YSL tie for his birthday. Fancy gift for a seventeen-year-old, no?" I queried.

"And a little stuffy. There are younger brands out there, surely."

"Right? I figured that the Lexus was Lucas's too. You don't think—" I began.

"Dinah bought it for him?" Beefa thought for a moment. "You think they've been in flagrante delicto?"

"I'm starting to. Yes. If that means banging. You're so fancy for a barbarian."

"I'm a mystery. Wrapped in a conundrum. Wrapped in bacon," said Beefa dryly.

I looked at Beefa squarely in the eye. "Get the feeling there's a five-meter croc below the surface?"

"If that means we haven't been told the whole story? Yes. But we can't leave these kids to fend for themselves."

I looked back toward the motel. "You're right. I hate it when you're right."

DANIEL HAD PASSED OUT, but his breathing and heartbeat were strong. After paying Bronson with some of Beefa's jerky, I plied Lisa with chamomile tea from the room's beverage caddy until she gradually fell asleep. I gave Liana all the coffee there was. Beefa took his cue to keep watch at the front window and I spoke with the older of Dinah's daughters in hushed tones.

"So, are you and Daniel ... involved?" I asked, leaning back against the mini-fridge, my ass already numb from the carpet-tiled floor.

"Does that mean ... dating?" she quizzed, slumped against the foot of Daniel's bed.

"Yeah. Translated from Old-ese. It means dating," I replied.

"We sort of were. I don't know. He likes me, I think," she said, running her painted fingers through her chocolate-colored locks.

"You seemed very upset when we found you."

"You saw. It was horrible."

"Sure was." I tightened my ponytail and massaged the sides of my skull. "Liana. I know this is hard, but I need you to tell me what happened exactly. So me and my beefy associate can go and get Lucas."

"Uncle Gideon..." Liana looked back at her sleeping sister. "He followed us down here. He came for Lucas. He hates Lucas."

"Why is that?"

Liana looked over her shoulder once more, then back at her lap. "I don't know."

Bad acting, Liana. I flicked through my notes. "The picture. The picture at your house—the one of you, Lisa, your mother and father. There's another man beside you all."

"That's him." Liana shivered.

I remembered the man in the photo: he had short hair—bleached blonde. Any wonder I didn't note a family resemblance. He was also broad and tall, with deep-set eyes. Not the kind of guy you'd want to rub the wrong way. I rubbed Lisa's arm. "It's okay. We're here to protect you. Where would he have taken Lucas? Back to Sydney?" I asked gently.

Bronson waddled over to Liana and nudged her with his meaty head as though he were urging an answer out of her. "Probably just somewhere ... where they could talk, or something?" said Liana as though *she* were asking *me*.

"Talk? Liana, he slashed Daniel with a knife—a bloody big one, I'd wager."

"No."

"No?"

"It wasn't meant to be like this, okay?" Liana was losing her cool.

"Wasn't meant to be like what?" I countered, on the verge of losing mine too.

"Radio-silence people," whisper-shouted Beefa. "We gotta' blip on our twelve."

Liana looked at me with a panicked but baffled expression. "There's someone outside," I clarified in a quiet voice.

Bronson knew not to bark (mama raised him well) and I carefully crawled over to Beefa's position. He pointed at the corner of the window as he lifted the blinds cautiously. I looked out. Outside, a tall, thin man in black jeans and a tattered gray jumper, stalked the carpark with an off-kilter gait. His limp, black hair hung over his eyes, brushing his bony nose with every step. Though, his booted feet barely seemed to touch the gravel.

Beefa tugged at my sleeve and I looked down to see him patting his belt. Then he pointed back outside. I knew Beef well enough to know what that meant: I looked straight at our prowler's waistline and saw a bulge there. He was carrying a gun.

Who the hell was this guy and how did he know where to find us? I had a hunch or two, of course, but none of them were pleasant. I felt a surge of anger at that moment: anger that me and Beefa had been sold up the river into a situation we'd not been appraised of. Bloody rich twats.

I let the anger flow through me; I knew I was going to need that rage injection and I was going to need it sooner rather than later.

"Lisa?" whispered our intruder through the door. Lisa sat up immediately—remember those possession movies I mentioned? I motioned for her to stay silent.

The front door knob began to jiggle, and I'll be honest, the contents of my stomach began to whirlpool. I wanted so much to reach for my big bag o' pills that I felt physical pain. The agony worsened when Limp-Hair began picking the lock.

Beefa was on his feet in an instant and I dragged myself up on shaky knees. I led Liana over to Lisa—who was now standing and rocking on her heels—and had them huddle together as best I could. I pulled the knife from my ankle-sheathe as Beefa stood there with his arms by his sides. I could feel pulses of excitement emanating off his broad back like heat waves over hot tarmac. What can I say—the man's an animal.

The door swung open revealing the slim silhouette of our guest. He pointed his already drawn weapon—a nasty-looking sawn-off shotgun—but Beefa was on him like a pit-bull. Beef grabbed the gun and jerked it back and to Limp-Hair's credit, he held onto the thing with grim determination. I rounded Beefa's bulk and slammed a shin into Limp-Hair's side. Repeatedly. The skinny prick didn't seem to register the pain of my well-placed kicks.

Beef pulled at the weapon with one almighty tug that sent Limp-Hair swinging from one side of the room to the other like a marionette, yet he held onto that bloody shotgun. Bronson latched onto the attacker's leg, tearing into it with so much gusto, his paws left the ground. Limp-Hair kicked him off and Bronson released a little 'yip' as he rolled across the floor, coming to a stop when he hit the bathroom door. That's when I saw red. I jumped onto the mini-fridge and propelled myself at the bastard, my knife held up over my head like some kind of berserker. Limp-Hair—still playing tug-o-war with Beef—threw his body to one side. I glanced off him, only landing a rudimentary slash to his gaunt cheek. I tumbled, righted myself, and came back at him from behind.

I drew back my arm, ready to unleash one hell of a stabbing, when I felt a sickening thud to the back of my skull. There were popping lights in my field of vision that I knew weren't there and I felt myself sliding into darkness. The last thing I heard was Beefa yelling out: "Motherfucker!" Then, nothing.

THE LIGHT HURT MY EYES and someone had re-routed a commuter train through my head, but other than that, I felt peachy. Bronson jumped onto the bed and licked my face. I couldn't help but giggle. Giggling hurt. Everything hurt. I looked about to see Beefa straightening my bedclothes and Liana huddled on the floor next to me. Hazarding a turn of my tortured head left, I saw Daniel in the other bed, right where we'd left him. I didn't see Lisa or Limp-Hair; lucky for both of them.

I'm not proud when I tell you that I scanned the room frantically for my coat, which had been thoughtfully removed from my person. Spotting it hanging from a wall-hook—the side pocket still swollen with painkillers—I breathed a sigh of relief. And I felt Beefa making a mental note of it.

"Lisa did this," I stated rather than asked.

"Yes," confirmed Liana. "Smashed a lamp on your head."

"You went down," began Beefa. "I lost focus. Released my grip." Beefa's face was overcome with something. Was it shame? Shame that he'd failed to protect me? "The thin man trained his weapon on me, then Lisa just grabbed his hand and off they fucked. Into the night."

I looked at Liana. "You're scared of her, aren't you? Last night you were looking to her before answering my questions."

"When we were younger, she always took charge. Always got her way. I was always told I was too quiet and that I would never amount to much." Liana's eyes filled with tears. Uncle Gideon liked her better than me. That's the problem."

"What problem is that?" asked Beefa.

Liana didn't answer.

My eyes met Beef's and I shot him a look that I hoped communicated my need to head up the interrogation.

"What about your father, Liana?" I asked.

"Our father?" she repeated. "He's dead."

"Dead? Your mother didn't mention that," I blurted.

"And we're sorry to hear it," added Beefa with a rebuke-filled glance aimed my way.

"Yes. Of course, we are," I said quickly. "It was recent? His passing?"

"Just ... It was a couple of weeks ago," said Liana, as she brought her knees up to her chest.

"That recent?" I said.

"Lisa..." began Liana.

"Yes?" I urged.

Liana spoke slowly. "Our uncle's evil. *She* might be worse."

Chapter Six

I wasn't happy that Beefa—courageous as he is—offered to investigate a lead on Liana's say-so. She'd told us (after much convincing) that there was a compound nearby; one that belonged to their church. In fact, it was this apparently 'safe-place' that drew them to the south coast. *The Immaculata*. It means untouched. Pure. Whole. Ironic that this was the name of a religion that uncle Gideon not only belonged to, but, according to Liana, served as some sort of elder within.

I paced the motel room floor as Liana dutifully tended to Daniel. He was opening his eyes sporadically and her face was the first thing he saw each time. I hope that was some source of comfort for the guy—he needed it. It was during one of those doe-eyed displays, that I took the opportunity to slip into the bathroom and down my own dose of comfort: ten pills with a couple more for good luck. I finished off the packet Charles had prescribed for me and only had to take a few from the motherlode in my jacket pocket. The ones I'd stolen off of Checked-Shirt were good. *Very* good.

I flipped through my notes as I re-entered the main living area. The codeine was working: I was beginning to feel more functional. I picked up some of the burnt toast delivered to the room as part of the bountiful breakfast we found left on a tray at the front door at some point during the wee hours. I offered some stale-looking cereal to Liana and she declined. Understandable. I threw a piece of what passed as bacon in the air and Bronson caught it. As he chewed, he looked up at me with an expression that was half gracious—half insulted. The 'fresh' coffee was welcome—even if it was kinda' watery. My mind started to grasp the basic outline of the whole sorry mess we now found ourselves in.

"So just one more thing," I began, turning my attention to Liana whilst employing my best Columbo voice. Shit like that amuses me and I was keen for a distraction. "Lisa is Gideon's favorite, yeah?"

"Yes," replied Liana, with a hurt expression.

"She was complicit in Lucas's abduction?" I queried.

"Yes."

"Her and Lucas weren't dating?" I asked.

"Not really."

I massaged my forehead. Extracting information from a teenage girl was like clearing out Bronson's blocked anal gland—which I'd done on more than one occasion and it was much more pleasant than the current line of questioning. "What am I missing here, Liana?" I spoke through a long sigh.

"Lucas was running away. He and Daniel are mates, so Daniel offered to go with him," said Liana. Hallelujah!

"Running away from Gideon. Right. Got that bit. Now, why?"

Liana stood up and walked over to me. She spoke in a whisper. "Gideon thought that Lucas and Mum were ... doing it," she said before checking that Daniel wasn't fully awake.

"I knew it!" I exclaimed before placing a finger over my own lips like I was telling myself to shut up.

"You did?" asked Liana.

"Yeah. I'm *that* good. So, Lucas is busted," I held up my open palms. "Allegedly, sleeping with Dinah. Gideon goes nuts—his brother, your father, has recently passed away. A fair reaction. What's not fair is hunting the boy down and taking him at knife-point after slashing his best friend to ribbons."

"He didn't." Liana's head turned like it was on a swivel. Daniel sat up awkwardly, wincing at the sudden flood of pain in his side. "Who are you?"

"One: I'm Zady. Liana's mother sent me," I said, paying keen attention to Daniel's reaction. His eyelids fluttered involuntarily at the mention of Dinah. Noted. "Two: nice to meet you properly. Also, be careful not to tear your stitches. I worked hard on those."

"Okay. Thanks for fixing me up," said Daniel. Polite kid. I liked him already.

"So, who cut you up, Daniel?" I asked.

Daniel's eyes met Liana's and I placed myself between them. No more bloody exchanged glances!

"Lisa," Daniel said, as his gaze dropped to his lap.

"Fuck. We're all fucked!" cried Liana from behind me.

"Why would she do that?" I pressed, moving in for the kill—figuratively, of course.

"Gideon took Lucas. He had this big-ass knife. I tried to stop him. Lisa came at me like a wild animal. Gideon threw her the knife, like they were some fucked up tag-team, and she took me down. We were wrestling and shit, rolling around. It was like she was keeping me pinned down while Gideon legged it back to his car with Luke."

"Taken down by a small girl," I teased. Not proud of it.

"I haven't realized my full-strength-potential yet. Anyway, she was crazy! Like something out of..." Daniel searched for an appropriate comparison. 'Say it!' I thought. "The Exorcist!" he blurted. 'Yes!' Knew I liked this kid for a reason.

"I nearly got the better of her. That's when she stuck me like a pig."

"So, you're running from Gideon. And you take Lisa and Liana with you?" I asked incredulously.

"Lisa insisted," added Liana.

"Gideon's lackey. Makes sense. She messaged that Limp-Haired prick, didn't she?" I seethed.

"Probably," said Liana.

"Dinah's not only frantic about Lucas—now she's worried about her daughters. Which is where I come in. Did mummy dearest know that Lisa was a bad seed?" I asked Liana.

"Doubt it. Leese is way manipulative," Daniel weighed in.

"Also, there's something else you should know—" began Liana.

Bronson trotted to the door, moments before it flew open, revealing a wide-eyed Beefa. "You gotta' come with me, Z!"

I HATED LEAVING LIANA and Daniel alone in that room. They were under strict instructions to keep the door locked. Bronson stayed as my representative and bodyguard. My heart pounded when I thought of him in that room without me. I looked out the truck window, at the rural properties whizzing by as me and Beef sped to our destination. It soothed me a little. Just a little.

"My recce mission yielded results. That Liana was right about the compound," said Beefa with trademark intensity. He often did 'recce', or 'reconnaissance missions' when we worked together—which was way too rarely in my opinion. It felt bloody good to have someone like Beefa in my corner. Especially when the world we'd been plunged into was so weird. End of reverie.

"What did you see there?" I asked.

"Not much. At first," Beefa said with a grim expression.

"I'm not going to like this, am I?"

"Look at it like a fascinating twist in our little narrative," said Beef, turning off the main road onto a dirt one.

"Fine. Do go on."

"There was an ordinary looking church building. A large house with a dormitory wing. It looked deserted. Then I saw it. I thought it was just a barn initially. On closer inspection, it was more of a—"

Something struck the side of the truck and we skidded. I thought it was just gravel and I wondered why Beefa was ducking down and urging me do the same. Then the second impact made it clear: we were being shot at. Bullets struck the driver's side and Beefa indicated that I should open my door, so I wasted no time in complying. We piled out of the truck and onto the ground. Beefa waved an arm toward a thick oak tree just a few meters away. I held up a hand—one, two, three more shots, then a pause. Fucker was reloading. "Go!" I yelled.

We ran for cover just before a hail of bullets struck the tree's trunk. When the next pause came, I hazarded a look. I couldn't see the source of the attack, just some rusted barrels stacked to form a make-shift barrier. Did they shoot at folks a lot out here? Not real godly, if you ask me.

After what felt like an eternity of me sticking my head out like a living target, I saw the top of a head, covered in dark hair. Limp hair. I withdrew.

"It's the twat who came for Lisa," I whispered to Beefa.

"Must have got wind of my earlier visit. I'm guessing this guy is Gideon's personal enforcer," replied Beef.

"What kind of bible-thumping outfit needs an enforcer?"

"The kind with a penchant for human sacrifice," drawled Beef.

"Say that again," I prompted.

"After we're done being shot at."

"I'm on board. What's the plan?" I asked.

Beefa didn't answer. He just disappeared. I looked out to see my fellow not-so-Hidden-Hand propelling his bulk toward Limp-Hair's position. He vaulted the barrel-wall before smashing the skinny prick back through it. Limp-Hair tried to point his rifle at Beef, but my good friend was having none of it this time. Beefa kicked his assailant in the face and snatched the weapon away, tossing it aside like a child's toy. Beef was suddenly astride Limp-Hair's chest, hitting him with alternating left and right hooks. I'm a fan of a little ground-and-pound and Beef didn't disappoint.

Beefa materialized beside me after scooping up the rifle. "AR-15," he said, examining the weapon. "Reliable enough. Good for spreading the word of our lord."

"I'm not a fan of guns, Beef," I said.

"I know, Z. Let's hang onto it until we've seen this thing out. Then it's gone. Deal?"

I looked away then back at Beefa. "Sure," I said unconvincingly.

"I've zip-tied Limpy's hands and feet. Now we've just gotta' pin down this Gideon character. I'm in the mood for punching a fucker," said Beef.

I nodded and we took off for the barn in question. The pit of my stomach soured and I thought, for a moment, that I would see my watery coffee and burnt toast again. I breathed deeply as we darted in and out of cover and pushed back the waves of nausea through sheer force of will.

The barn loomed up like a wooden behemoth, squatting over the land and infecting it. Even the woodwork on the huge front doors had the look of cruel teeth in an open mouth. I hated it immediately. "I climbed the loading hoist over here," said Beefa, pointing to the north side of the building. "I just hope we're not too late." We crept along the barn's face and then around the corner, staying low all the while.

Beefa slung the rifle over his shoulder and gave me a boost and I shot up the rope toward the steel pully overhead. I had to swing gradually closer to the opening near the roof, lolling back and forth like the pendulum of a bloody grandfather clock. I grabbed the opening's sill and steadied myself before leaping for it. My legs dangled over the edge and I scraped my chest and belly on the way in. It was all I could do not to swear at the pain, not clear on who or what would be awaiting me in the dark of the barn's bowels.

When Beefa appeared next to me, we skirted the mezzanine and looked over its edge into the barn proper. There were no hay bales or tractor parts. The stuff of good, decent farming folk was conspicuous by its absence. Instead, the space was lit by candles—lots of them. Against the far wall, a statue of shiny, black marble reached up toward the rafters.

I looked into its soulless eyes and felt lost all of a sudden: like their inky vacancy would suck me in forever. Silly, I know. I chanced a closer look, inching forward on my hands and knees and I had to blink repeatedly to ensure what I was seeing was really there.

Lisa stood in the room's center—clad in a black gown—holding a silver tray in front of her. On the tray were a knife with a silver hilt, a metal goblet, and a small wooden box. Next to her stood a tall man wearing a black robe. A man with broad shoulders and bleached hair. Gideon. His head was bowed as though in prayer to the great sculpture that towered over both parties. This was some wicked shit.

As I leaned in as far as I dared, I caught sight of another. A young lad, restrained by ropes and laid out on a stone table. An altar. He wept and implored thinly. He sounded exhausted, as though he'd been begging for his freedom, his life, for hours on end. My heart ached for him. I looked at Beefa—he was pale. I'd never seen the color drain out of him like that. I was scared that the bravest man I knew was scared.

Lisa placed the tray down near Lucas's feet. Gideon placed a hand on the boy's forehead and Lisa mumbled. I could only make out one phrase: "With this offering do we honor our lord and savior—Ba'al—the beginning and the end." Then she cut out Lucas's tongue.

Chapter Seven

Lisa placed Lucas's severed tongue in the ornate wooden box atop the silver tray. Afterward, she looked at her fingers—coated in blood—and licked them clean as her victim writhed like a worm on the altar. Beefa pointed the rifle at the ground between Lisa and her uncle and flicked the safety off. I gently placed a hand on his arm and shook my head when Beef looked my way. I didn't want the pair to flee, in case they made for Daniel and Liana, still at the motel. I looked about the place, finally spotting a ladder that led down to the front of the barn—behind Lisa and Gideon.

I could take Lucas's muted screams no more; I made for the ladder, quietly descending into the hellish scene below as Beefa followed. I dropped onto the hay-lined floor and crouched like a cat. Beefa lowered himself just next to me and signaled for me to secure Lisa as he was neutralizing Gideon. I knew he'd have used the word 'neutralizing', like a big, old army-geek, if we were communicating verbally. Together we moved toward our respective targets, low and silent, both advancing at the same speed. Lucas's thrashing and grunting did a decent job of masking any unintentional noise on our part and our quarry showed no sign of twigging to our gradual approach.

Lisa picked up the knife that lay next to the wooden box. She held it aloft and looked up as she called out in a voice that made my neck-hairs stand up.

"We offer this tainted meat, as ransom for our sinful state. Please bless us as we drink his blood and enslave his soul, Ba'al our king, God, and savior!" I was almost on her when she spoke again. "For the crimes of adultery with my weakling mother, and the murder of my beloved father, I sentence you to death eternal—Lucas Evan Leary!"

I froze and my eyes met Beefa's. 'Murder?' I mouthed silently. I suddenly wished I hadn't.

Gideon spun around and dive-bombed Beefa—his rifle skidding across the room—as Lisa flew at me, her jagged blade slashing ferociously. Poor Daniel hadn't stood a chance: the girl was wiry, strong, and as vicious as the day is long. I stole a glimpse sideways and saw Beef copping a headbutt, followed by a crazy-ass bite to the neck. I wasn't doing much better. Lisa pulled at my hair and pressed her blade into my neck—I could feel the skin about to give way. Shit was getting dire. Then a crash to my left, as Gideon was thrown into the wall. Classic Beefa. Lisa was distracted—her attention drawn by her uncle's cursing—so I delivered a knee to her crotch. She wailed and fell sideways, curling up and rocking on her back like a fussy infant.

Beefa bolted for the gun and I scooped up Lisa's blade and ran for Lucas. His eyes were crazed and he looked terrified, until he realized that I was cutting his bonds and not his throat. The sound of crashing caught my attention and I turned to see a steel candelabra hit the ground, sending lit candles in all directions. The hay-covered ground caught fire and flames soon licked at the wooden barn-walls. Hellish indeed. I turned back to Lucas, secure in the knowledge that Beefa would certainly reclaim his weapon—giving us the upper hand. Lucas's eyes were wide again. Mine were soon closed.

GROGGY AND DISORIENTED, I hazarded a look around. I saw Lisa's stupid face slowly pull into focus and my heart sank. The upper hand! When did we lose the upper hand?

"You nutted me again?" I asked and Lisa nodded with a big old shit-eating grin.

I was getting sick of being knocked out cold—by the same bitch, no less.

I was suddenly aware of the bite of rope at my wrists and I tried to move my legs but they were in the same boat. I was laid flat—my arms under me—with Beefa to my right, similarly trussed but unconscious. Thick trucker straps at my chest and thighs, held me down flat. The bastards had taken my coat (and my pills) and in the small of my back—where my shirt had ridden up—I could feel the cool metal of a table-top. At least it wasn't an altar; it was more like something you'd find in a morgue. Comforting. A severe-looking face came way too close to mine.

"You're not welcome..." began Gideon. He'd ditched the robe—opting for a similar dark suit to that in his photo back at the Rose Bay house. He opened a wallet. My wallet. He looked at me before eyeballing something inside of it. "... Zady Proya," he spat. "You've failed. You failed to read the situation. You failed to retrieve my whore of a sister-in-law's lover."

Lisa stared straight into my eyes as she lifted a goblet to her mouth and drained it. Afterward, she wiped crimson from her lips. Blood. Lucas's blood. I struggled against my binds as she cackled. "Mmm... salty," she said.

"You killed him?"

"He was executed, not killed," Lisa shot back.

"My brother, Ezekiel, was incensed when he found Lucas in his wife's bed. They fought. My brother fell and cracked his skull open and at that moment—"

"—the infernal sinner, Lucas, died as well," interjected Lisa. "He was as good as dead the moment he defiled Mother."

"Ba'al demanded an offering and he has received it. He will soon receive two more," said Gideon.

"You'll choke on our blood, you insane fuckers!" I spat.

"Oh, not you two. We have some other rites planned for you both," said Gideon, waving a hand over a veritable arsenal of sharp instruments on the table beside him. "The Rites of Cleansing. You'll be kept alive for quite some time as we visit upon you the Trials of the Flesh. But as for the additional offerings, you have also failed Lisa's sister and that idiot that she took down. What's his name?" he asked of Lisa.

"Daniel," she offered.

"Biblical," said Gideon. "Very good."

"Nothing about this is biblical!" I cried.

"The scriptures have hidden gems that few have mined," began Gideon. "I founded the inner circle of The Immaculata on that basis. Yet, few are pure enough to stand before Ba'al."

I tried to keep the lunatic talking as I tested my restraints for weaknesses. It was proving difficult, both listening to the tripe Gideon was unloading, and finding loose spots in the knots about my wrists. "Liana was offered membership to your little grubby club?" I asked.

"She's scared of bloody everything!" yelled Lisa. "But she'll come around. When she beholds Daniel's judgement."

"I'll go and fetch them," oozed Gideon. "You stay and watch over the wicked." He kissed Lisa's forehead and she giggled stupidly as he turned and disappeared into the corridor outside the door.

My eyes scanned the place and I quickly drank in my surroundings. I guessed they'd dragged us into the main house. The room was tiled and I swore I could see traces of blood in the grout—this was not their first foray into torture. Tortured. I was NOT in the mood to be tortured. It wasn't just me and Beef copping the short end, what about those poor kids: completely unaware of Gideon's approach? Why, oh why, hadn't I left Liana with some cash—told her to relocate? Maybe she'd already thought of that. I would have prayed right then and there, if I'd thought it would have helped.

"Why don't we play a game while uncle's away?" said Lisa in a sickening sing-song voice. She circled me and plucked a dirty-looking scalpel from the selection of surgical instruments.

"Why don't you get fucked?" I said. Not my best burn ever, but it's all that came to mind in the moment.

Lisa slapped my face. "Rude," she spat. She sauntered over to the far wall and pulled a rubber apron off a cast iron hook. She put the scalpel in her mouth (most unhygienically) as she tied the apron-strings around her slender waist. She spat the scalpel back into her hand before speaking again. "How about you guess something about me, and if it's true, I'll fetch you a glass of water?"

"And if I'm wrong?" I asked, already guessing the bloody answer.

"I get to cut something off."

My vision blurred slightly. "Oh, I'm bored already. Get on with it!" I yelled.

"Great!" she said, stamping her feet on the ground. I looked down and noticed for the first time that she wore clunky buckled shoes. Where did she get them from? 1785? It struck me as creepy for some reason. "Let's begin!"

"Whatever," I said. "Wow... Soooo much to work with here." My eyes found Beefa and I did my best to will him conscious. It didn't work. "I'm going to go ahead and guess that you weren't just obeying orders when you accompanied Lucas on his little escape." Lisa's face dropped; I had her. "You liked him. You have a thing for rich boys. Entitled little twats who can afford to offer you the life to which you've become accustomed, et bloody cetera."

Lisa grimaced. Then she cut off my right earlobe. "You motherfucker!" I cried. "I was right, wasn't I?"

Lisa looked at the bloody chunk of flesh before throwing it over her shoulder. "He's not rich," she said.

"Okay. Comfortable. Is that a less gaudy word for it?" I asked.

"He was one of Mother's wayward youths. She found him through her stupid charity." Lisa looked away. "She was more concerned with the comings and goings of street-scum than she was with her own family.

"Oh, don't give me the mummy-doesn't-love-me-so-I'm-a-rancid-devil-worshipping-little-cunt routine!" I needed her to come unstuck. I'm a little saltier than a goblet of delicious blood when it comes to swearing, but the C-word erupting from my mouth surprised even me.

Lisa's lower jaw jutted forward and she jabbed the scalpel into my forearm, dragging the blade slowly down to my wrist. I didn't give her the satisfaction of a scream, but shit, did it hurt. I chewed on the inside of my mouth and tasted copper. I inhaled and exhaled. But I didn't scream.

Blood streamed from the wound. If she'd hit an artery, at least I'd rob her of the satisfaction of using me like a plaything. I felt bad about leaving Beefa, and Bronson—my dear little Bronson. He was at the motel with the kids. Ba'al wouldn't be able to save Gideon from me if he hurt my little baby. Of course, that threat was predicated upon me surviving and somehow escaping, so... kinda' empty as threats go.

My thoughts turned back to Lisa's ranting. "Lucas was poor? That's why it was okay to kill him?" I demanded. "Cos' he came from nothing?"

"The way you defend him—it's because you're trash too," she drawled. "Coming out here, sticking your brown little face into things you don't understand." There it was. I added casual racism to the laundry list of reasons to kick her lily ass. "Putting your hand out for cash, delivered by your betters. In the good old days, you might have served me minted tea on my plantation house patio."

I paused for a moment and swallowed my white-hot rage. I was not going to let my voice quiver. Not one bit. "If I'm trash, you're hot liquid excrement, girlfriend," I countered calmly.

The scalpel's point hovered over my forehead. "Which eye is your favorite? You know, which one can you *really* not do without?" Lisa said with a smile.

A loud smash ended our little back and forth as it shook the entire building. Lisa stood bolt upright, her eyes fixed on the doorway like a spooked dog. She began to inch forwards, the scalpel held out in front of her. "Lord? Have you answered my prayers? Have you come?" she asked of the nothingness in a hoarse whisper. "Ba'al my one true God ... Take me!" Lisa slashed at her wrists with the blade. "*My* blood is *your* blood!"

A thick lump of wood came down on Lisa's head. Hard. She fell like a dropped blanket. "It is. And I wish it wasn't," said a voice from the shadows.

Chapter Eight

The figure standing over me looked inhuman under the glow of flickering fluorescent lights. Not overly tall. Slight of build. Female. She discarded the plank of wood she'd used to knock Lisa flat on her ass and began pulling at my restraints.

"There's a knife tucked away at my right ankle," I said to my savior. "Liana."

She pulled the blade and began work on the straps. "Daniel is under your dog's guard. I had to come. I had a bad feeling," said Liana.

"Cut quickly. Your uncle is en route to the motel right this minute," I said. My words came out more calmly than I'd expected.

Finished with the binds that secured me to the table, Liana began work on the rope at my ankles. I sat up awkwardly—pins and needles accosting my extremities—and presented my wrists.

"You'd better take care of that," said Liana, eyeing the gash that ran the length of my forearm.

"You'd better hogtie that sister of yours. You weren't kidding about her," I countered.

Liana nodded solemnly and I hugged her. "Christ, I'm happy to see you."

"Go," she said before pulling open a drawer in a sideboard and handing me a clean, rolled bandage.

"Wake Beefa. He'll look out for you while I'm gone," I said before leaving the torture room, glad to put it behind me.

I quickly wrapped my arm as I jogged. As I rounded the corner I was confronted with sheer chaos. Liana had driven the Lexus to the compound and simply rammed it into the front of the main building. I wasted no time sliding across the hood (pretty cool, if I do say so myself) and climbing into the driver's seat through the smashed window. The keys were still in the ignition and the engine was idling. The transmission sounded a little rough, but I managed to convince the thing to reverse and before long, I was barreling down the dirt path, slowing when I came to Beefa's truck. There was no sign of Limp-Hair. Gideon must have cut him loose and taken him with. Fuck.

I was grateful for Lucas's car and its very respectable grunt as I sped toward the motel. My heart drummed my chest the whole way and my head swam. I was worried about Daniel but hand on heart, I was more concerned for little Bronson. Images of his brave wee face flooded my brain as I wove through the traffic. I could have cheered when The Castle on the Coast's sign loomed up on the horizon, but I didn't. My vision was already off-kilter. So much rage.

I skidded to a halt right in front of the hotel room's door and as I emerged, my heart sank. The door had been kicked in. I carelessly pushed through, not bothering to check for imminent danger, and I had the hide to be shocked when Limp-Hair kicked me straight into the mini fridge. I locked eyes with Gideon who had his big old mitts wrapped around Daniel's throat. The boy's face was almost blue—I was running out of time. Don't let me lose another one. Please.

Limp-Hair came at me with another kick to the chest but I managed to grab hold of his ankle in the process. I held on tight and twisted with everything I had. I smirked when I heard the sickly sound of ligaments tearing, and I felt a rush of adrenaline as I brought my foot up, hammering his genitals so ferociously, he vomited all over his crappy gray jumper. I threw Limp-Dick (sure, I renamed him) aside and hurled myself at Gideon. That's when I wished Beef was with me.

The man took his hands from Daniel's neck and concentrated them on me. He threw me on the other bed and sat on my legs, punching my face repeatedly. I could taste and smell blood as he rained blow upon blow on my cheekbones, mouth, and nose. My head lolled about and that's when I saw my worst nightmare made manifest: Bronson—laid out on his side on the floor. He wasn't moving. My vision blurred, and not from Gideon's punches.

I reached up and grabbed the bastard by the scruff of his neck and yanked him over me. He hit the floor between the bed and the wall and I could hear him immediately scrambling to right himself. I rolled myself to the right and tumbled to my feet, holding up my fists like a prize-fighter at the end of a boxing film. This was the scene in the movie where I proved how much more heart I had than my opponent. Even I didn't buy that level of extreme self-bullshittery in that moment. Chances were, I was about to buy the farm. I was simply too pissed off to die.

I blinked the blood out of my eyes, catching sight of the rocket-powered left coming my way just in the nick of time. I knocked it off-course with all the force I could pump into my right arm, countering with my trademark knee to the crotch, followed by a jab to the throat. When Gideon was nice and disoriented, I brought a boot up to his ribs and tenderized them with one, two, three kicks that would have sent a man of average build reeling. This was not a man of average build. He came back at me with a headbutt that had me seeing stars. I wanted to drop. Close my eyes and sleep. Then I heard the sweetest sound I've heard in my life. Ever.

Snorting and snarling preceded a startlingly vicious assault on Gideon's calf muscle. Seriously—I heard muscle being torn from bone, and I loved every second. Bronson's face was barely visible: obscured by thick fonts of blood as he bit, ripped and tore his mama's attacker with extreme prejudice. Gideon's face was the color of a bedsheet in a far cleaner motel. I grabbed the man by the shoulders and threw him onto the ground with Bronson still attached. Sitting astride his broad chest I laughed maniacally before commencing a session of face-smashing old uncle Gideon would never forget. Told you: I love me some ground-and-pound.

I CAN'T TELL YOU HOW long I sat on Gideon's chest, both of us looking like something in the butcher shop window. I just stared into space, letting everything wash over me at once. To be honest, I wasn't even concerned whether the man was alive or dead at that point—I just sort of zoned out. Gradually I became aware of voices that sounded like they were coming from miles away. In a more rational corner of my brain, I wondered whether someone had called the cops. I'd certainly have a lot of explaining to do. Then I heard the familiar baritone that I longed for.

"Liana, check Daniel's pulse. Z! Can you stand?" said Beefa, with an endearing amount of concern in his usually monotone voice.

"Stand," I repeated, as though the word were alien to me. "Yes. Let's try that," I responded.

Beef helped me to my feet, his touch gentle, like he was handling a hurt dove. "Easy does it," he said softly.

"Are you okay, Beefa?" I asked, suddenly painfully aware of my surroundings.

"Better than him," replied Beef, gesturing at Gideon's swollen face. "Impressive," he added, with no hint of irony.

"Thanks. I'm happy with how it went," I replied.

"Found this," said Beefa as he handed me my trench coat.

"You're the absolute shit!" I exclaimed, taking the garment and discreetly feeling around for the pills in my pocket. Still there. Bloody spectacular!

"We'll talk about its contents later?" said Beef.

I threw in a nonchalant: "Mm-hm" as I ducked down and searched Gideon for my wallet. Found it.

"He's alive!" cried Liana, hugging Daniel tearily.

"What do you want to do about the mess?" asked Beefa.

"Did you bring ... Liana's sister?" I whispered.

"Yeah. Bound and stowed in the back of the truck. Covered her in a blanket so no one would see."

"I'm half tempted to leave the little witch here with these assholes. Let the cops deal with the lot of them," I said.

"Not your style, Z."

"I'm all outta' style," I replied mirthlessly.

"We take the girls back to their mother. Get Daniel back safely too. Fulfil our end of the bargain," said Beef.

"And these tossers?" I asked, way too spent to formulate decisions.

"We leave them. Let the motel call the police. By the time anyone traces anything back, we'll be out of the picture. I've taught you how to lay low effectively. We might need to make ourselves scarce for a time," whispered Beef.

"Might be wise," I said. "And Lucas?"

"Cops'll work their way back to the compound. An anonymous phone tip off might help in that regard," said Beef.

"At this point, that's sounding like the only viable option."

Beefa casually walked over to Limp-Hair, knelt down, and delivered a ground shaking punch to the back of the man's head. "He was starting to stir," he said by way of explanation.

"Bronson!" I yelled as my lucidity hit a new high. I threw myself onto my behind and held my arms open wide. My little man waddled over and entered into a vigorous embrace. "Don't scare me like that again, little furry-butt!" I kissed him on the face until he emitted a sound not unlike the oinking of a pot-bellied pig—he does that when I get overly affectionate. Then I kissed him a little more.

"Okay troops—it's high time we were—" began Beefa.

"—Oscar Mike?" said Liana, beating him to the punch.

"You're picking up the lingo!" I commended. "I like this chick."

THE DRIVE BACK TO SYDNEY was quiet and direct—no unnecessary stops. Between trying to clean myself up with wet-wipes from Beef's glovebox and wrestling with what I was going to say to Dinah, I faded in and out. Lisa—sitting upright and still covered in a blanket—wriggled and dished out eye-wateringly vile insults for a time but then gave in to sleep. Daniel tried to make conversation with Beefa from his position in the back between the girls, but soon gave up after a half-dozen grunted responses. Liana just stared out of the window as far as I could see in my waking moments. Bronson snored and chased dream-bunnies on my lap and I really didn't want the journey to end. When we set down in Darkwood's driveway, I wanted to cry. So much awful shit had gone down and I wasn't sure I could contain my emotions on seeing Dinah for the first time since the insanity began.

My stomach boiled as I hit the front doorbell and I felt dizzy as soon as I heard the stir of footsteps coming up the long hallway. The door opened a crack and Dinah's sad little face appeared. There was no lip gloss this time and her scent was not sweet, in fact, she smelled largely unwashed. Her hair was all over the place and instead of designer couture, Dinah wore a stained dressing gown that may have been fashionable somewhere around the mid-fifties. When I'd first met her, she'd looked like a woman of maybe thirty-five. Now she looked like she was in her sixties. What a difference a couple of stress-filled days make. Any anger I was feeling on the way quickly drained out of me. I was happy to leave it at the door as I entered.

I'd asked Beefa to wait outside while I explained the basics of the situation as it stood. Dinah had trouble listening after I'd told her we had brought back her daughters in reasonable condish. I held her steady as I explained why one of them was trussed up like a Christmas goose but I don't think she got the message. She just burst out the door and demanded to see her babies and Beefa gently obliged.

Luckily it was dark when we carried Lisa and then Daniel into the house. Lisa was placed on her own bed and Daniel took up residence on the couch in the main living area. Once we were all inside and I'd convinced Dinah to give me some food for Bronson (I don't think he'd ever tried Foie Gras before), I asked Liana to pour her mother a drink. I waited until Dinah had taken a couple of decent slugs from her tumbler before I broke the news about Lucas. It was all there in her reaction: she'd loved the boy. I don't know where to start on the ethical angle of their relationship, but it was crystal clear that she'd cared for him very deeply. She basically fell off her chair when she absorbed the fact that he was dead. She wept as I relayed the edited version of what fate had befallen him, and she wailed when I told her that it was largely her most favored daughter at the bottom of it.

"What I don't understand…" I began, adopting my Columbo voice once again. "…is who made that phone call to you, Dinah."

"The what?" she asked thinly.

"The call. The one where the caller quoted the book of Romans. Indicated to you that dodgy things were afoot." My eyes met Beefa's for a moment.

"Don't worry about that for now, Mum," cooed Liana, hopping up to adjust her mother's cushions.

Vanessa, the maid, sauntered in out of the blue. I found it odd that she hadn't shown up as soon as she heard that her mistress had company. She just stood there, looking from Dinah, to me, and then back at Dinah.

"Mr. Gideon," she began. "Any news about Mr. Gideon?" she blurted.

"You may not be seeing him for some time," I replied.

Dinah lurched forward and sobbed a little at my remark. Vanessa sobbed harder. She ran from the room and I remembered the hickey on her neck from the day I took on this god-awful case. Gideon's handiwork no doubt. Had *she* made the call to Dinah? Why would she have done that? Was she so worried about her lover that she was moved to drum up some help? Get Dinah in a tizzy and start some kind of weird-ass ball rolling? I was too tired to piece it together. The maid had left but Dinah barely registered her departure. "Silly girl better see to those cobwebs," was all she said in a hoarse voice I could barely hear.

Liana abruptly cleared her throat. She looked at me, gesturing toward the hallway. At first, I thought she was suggesting that I'd upset her mother enough and that me, my dog, and my Beefa should leave. That was until I twigged that she wanted to speak to me privately. I feared for what I was about to learn next.

Chapter Nine

I locked eyes with Beef, wordlessly asking if he was okay with keeping watch over Daniel and Dinah. Daniel was in a deep sleep and Dinah was simply staring into space. Bronson lay with his hind legs sprawled out behind him; he looked like a Portuguese chicken. Beefa's expression told me that he'd rather be flossing with razor-wire than in the present company (save for my fur-baby), but he would stay for as long as needed. Such a good bear.

Liana led me to Lisa's room, her hips swaying as she walked. She had always moved so rigidly up until now. She suddenly seemed more relaxed. Peculiar, seeing as how the shit had really hit the proverbial of late. Was she gaining confidence, or dropping an assumed persona? Only time would tell.

We gathered at Lisa's huge antique bed and together we quietly removed her restraints. I was reticent at first—would the bitch lunge at me, I wondered? She simply sat up, rubbed her wrists and ankles, and hugged her sister. I realized then that I had no idea how their family dynamic worked. Was Lisa lulling Liana—and me—into a false sense of security before calling in reinforcements? The funny thing was, my hackles stayed lowered and I didn't have the sinking feeling in the pit of my stomach that I usually get before being double-crossed. Maybe she'd learned her lesson. Yeah and maybe a pig would fly right out of my ass.

As the pair whispered things to one another, I walked around the room and took it all in. There was a glass cabinet in the far corner of the substantial bedroom; it was filled with porcelain figurines of bunnies, badgers, and other English-looking woodland creatures. The walls were adorned with framed posters, not of movie stars or boybands, but of cartoon characters. There was something so odd about the infantile feel of the space. It was like a tour of Lisa's mind and what a mind it was.

A familiar odor suddenly caught my attention and I moved about, sniffing for it like a hound chasing a fox. Only, this fox smelled rotten. After looking back at the siblings still locked in quiet conversation, I approached what smelt like the culprit: a tall armoire that stood like a sentinel in the southern corner of the bedroom. That funk—what was it? When I'd first visited Dinah, I'd blamed the rotting cat food in the living area. Was dear little Lisa stowing pilchards in aspic in her wardrobe? It wouldn't have surprised me one bit after the traffic of the past couple of days.

I cautiously opened the door a little and was rewarded with a wave of awfulness that violated my nose with extreme prejudice. It was rot alright, but not the rot of pet chow: it was the stench of rotting pet.

"That's Amon," said Lisa casually.

I looked over my shoulder without actually making eye contact. "Lisa... Who is Amon?"

"He's a servant of Ba'al now," she replied flatly.

I looked into the darkness of the armoire, steeled myself, and threw the doors wide open. Hanging clothes were parted to accommodate an altar. An altar with fruit and cash and candles beneath it, and the severed head of a ginger cat sitting on top. "Where's the rest of the animal?" I asked in my best calm-mother-voice.

"Burned. An offering to the great one," Liana responded. I felt strange hearing her say something so callous. I thought she was meant to be the good one. Now my hackles were well and truly upright.

"Liana... I'm only going to ask you once—did you call your mother? Quote the bible at her? Get her all worked up?" I turned away from the grotesquerie of the altar and faced the sisters.

"Goodness, no. What a predictable twist that would make," she replied, caressing Lisa's hair as she spoke. The pair now sat on the edge of the four-poster bed. Hand in hand. "I allowed my little Li Li to do what I knew she would." Liana pinched Lisa's cheek as though she were nothing more than an incorrigible little scamp. "I knew she'd stir shit up."

"You *allowed* her to?" I repeated.

"When she was born..." Liana began, standing up and wandering toward me. "...Lisa was rock solid. Literally. They thought she was still born and they told mother to say hello and goodbye simultaneously. Silly cow prayed to god at first. Begged him to save her baby. Nothing happened."

"And then?" I goaded, knowing full well the answer.

"Then Father prayed to Ba'al," replied Lisa, as though reciting a story she'd told many a time before.

Liana nodded approvingly. "Lisa opened her eyes and began screaming after being dead for more than five minutes. Needless to say, she wasn't right in the head after that."

"I did the phone call," said Lisa. "I used a voice-changing app and I read from Romans."

"To what end? Why any of this?" I blurted. Frustrated and tired and fucked off by the whole sorry affair.

"You roughed up someone for a friend of mine once. Her name was Rachel. Not the sharpest tool in the shed, but a decent little soul. He was stalking her. Phoning her and jerking off as she yelled at him to stop. When he grabbed her one day after school, she searched the internet for help and came across you. I see him occasionally, wandering the streets. He has no teeth now." Liana stood strangely still as she spoke.

"I remember. So, you wanted your uncle taken care of?" I asked.

"I sent an anonymous email to Mother with your details. I couldn't handle the whole Lucas situation and Gideon on my own. I needed some dumb-ass muscle to get involved and do the heavy lifting. Problem is: you're not so dumb after all."

"Thanks?" I replied. "You wanted Lucas punished. I get that. You wanted it done somewhere remote. I get that too. What do you have against your uncle? You disapprove of the false-god worship?"

Liana's face hardened. "The only false-god is the one Mother puts her faith in. Ba'al is the light."

"The light that sanctions the killing of teenage boys?" I questioned, edging back toward the door.

"He punishes the evildoer. Rewards those who serve him," said Liana.

"You want to join the Inner Circle? But, what? They won't have you?" I teased.

"I don't want to join the Inner Circle. I want to run it." Liana ran her fingers through her dark hair as though the mere thought of leading the cult was a sensual pleasure.

When I reached the door handle, I grabbed it without turning away from Liana. She answered with a knife to my throat. "You won't call the cops. You won't squeal like the oinking pig that you are," she spat, her voice dripping with venom.

"Oh? And why's that?" I stalled.

"I know you. I know your friend. The Circle has eyes and ears all over. We'll find out where you hole up and do things to you that you can't possibly imagine. Maybe I'll place your little dog's head on an altar all of his own."

My eyes vibrated, my temples pumped, and my stomach heaved. I knocked the knife aside and picked Liana up by the scruff of her designer t-shirt. "You can fucking try," I spewed.

I threw her across the room—Beefa was rubbing off on me—and she landed against the foot of the bed. Lisa stood to attention and helped her sister up, the two of them advancing on me like vampires from a B-grade horror flick. I opened the door and barreled down the hallway, standing before the sleepy-looking Dinah with my hand outstretched.

"Payment please!" was all I could squeeze out of my mouth. My lips were still quivering with uncut rage.

"Oh, I have to find it," Dinah mumbled as she rose awkwardly and made for a lidded box that sat upon a walnut credenza. "Yes. I left it here."

Beefa hopped up—bringing Bronson to life in the process—and cast a cursory glance over Daniel. "He may need antibiotics," he said to Dinah as she produced a fat envelope.

"I'll see to it," she replied.

"Good luck with the Addams Family," I spat, grabbing the cash and making for the corridor without so much as a goodbye.

I could just make out Beef's military boots and Bronson's claws hitting the wooden floors over the pounding in my head. As the fresh night air hit my face and defeated the smell of decay, I was glad to put Darkwood and its inhabitants behind me. Though, I could feel them in my wake: crouched like gargoyles adorning a church. A church devoid of hope.

THE DRIVE HOME WAS tense. I kept looking at Beefa, his thick hands manipulating the steering wheel, shifting gears: the stuff of normalness. Nothing was normal now and it would never be again. I thought I was cynical and jaded before, but this ordeal had taken me to new lows. I craned my neck and looked at Bronson: asleep in the back seat.

"You gonna' tell me what happened in there?" asked Beefa. "You've been ... different since."

"One day. Once I digest the battery acid in my belly," I replied.

"That bad?"

"Let's just say that you're right about relocating," I said.

"I know a place on the Central Coast," offered Beef.

"Might need to make it interstate."

When we arrived at Beefa's place, I made a bee line for the artillery box in the kitchen and my phone. There were several missed calls from Dinah and the odd spam email for discounted anal bleaching, but little else. Beefa stopped packing food for a moment and our eyes met. He nodded and I found myself doing the very thing I'd been ordered not to. Ordered not to by a snot-nosed, entitled, evil teenaged princess. Fuck that.

I gave the police Darkwood's address and that of the motel where Gideon and Limp-Dick had probably put behind them by now. I detailed the location of the compound and laid out all that had happened without mention of Beefa or myself. They kept asking how I'd come to know about the things I described and I just kept talking. When I hung up, I felt a mixture of relief and panic. Hopefully the whole thing wouldn't come back to bite us in the ass like a scrappy bulldog. I dropped down onto my knees and scratched Bronson's head and Beef threw him a very generous eye-fillet.

"It'll go bad otherwise," said Beefa when I shot him an inquisitive look.

"Like Lisa and Liana," I replied.

"Let's leave them for dust," said Beefa. He'd heard what I'd revealed over the phone yet his face showed no surprise. I loved Beefa at that moment: he was the solid brick-wall of a human being I needed more than anything. I watched as he threw his duffel bag onto the floor before putting an arm out; Cockrates landed there. Beefa slid open the side door and raised his forearm and the cockatoo moonward. "Go on, mate. Time to rejoin polite society," he said.

I fancied, for an instant, that I saw a tear cascade into his thick, brown beard as the bird flew off into the night sky.

I pulled a weighty envelope from my pocket and threw it at the man and he deftly caught it. "What's this about?" he asked.

"That's what Dinah gave us before we left. Payment. You've more than earned it, big fella," I replied.

"This is too much," he countered.

"Don't get all excited. You'll be shouting me dinner for the next month."

"Done," he said. "But you'll be eating more protein and fewer carbs. Getting a little soft in the middle," he quipped, slapping his own firm belly.

"Prick!" I exclaimed with mock offense.

He grabbed my phone off me and dumped it into a metal bin, squirting it with lighter fluid, and setting the thing ablaze.

"Oscar Mike, Z!" said Beef.

I sighed. "Oscar fucken' Mike indeed," I replied.

Epilogue

Our little ragtag party: faithful bulldog, wannabe soldier, and whatever the hell I was trying to be, arrived at Devonport, Tasmania, a little worse for wear. As we exited the ship in Beef's truck and took in the surroundings, I was more than glad to put Darkwood, the New South Wales south coast and The Immaculata into a nice little box and bury it deep in my mind's recesses. For good with any luck. My body was sore. My spirit was sore. My heart and mind were in tatters. How had I gone from roughing up ruffians to witnessing human sacrifice and almost becoming one myself? Not to mention poor Beefa and Bronson. The two of them were eerily quiet and I knew our little misadventure had exacted a hefty toll on the both of them too.

Farmland rolled by and the early morning mist blanketed the hills and dales of the countryside. I wound down the window and thrust my hand out into the cool air. The fifteen or so painkillers I'd swallowed in one of the ship's pokey bathrooms had begun to plunge me into a comforting haze and the wind felt sensual as it whipped my face. Beefa hadn't mentioned my stash and I was grateful for it. He was able to articulate his disapproval with the odd gesture or look without ramming it down my throat.

We stopped for coffee and snacks en route to Launceston, our verbal exchanges brief but loaded with unspoken things. I fancied we could make a new start on the Apple Isle, maybe change our names. I toyed with chopping off my hair and dying it blonde. I'd have to relinquish my beloved trench coat too. Bugger. Would there even be work for a couple of try-hard mercenaries in this peaceful place? Perhaps we'd open a guest house where we'd welcome patrons with homemade bread, preserves, and bottles of local wine. Kids would pet Bronson's little head and Beefa would chop wood for the fireplace and fend off the advances of back-packers keen on romantic sojourns abroad. Me? I'd keep house and put violence and intrigue away for good. I'd get clean too. Settle for sips of port by the hearth and all the stuff of a normal life. Could I hack it?

The hours passed effortlessly. Time seemed like a nebulous concept that held little meaning. For some reason, my thoughts turned to the past—the deep past. I remembered pain and blood and a back operation that would have seen most confined to years of physical therapy. I'm not most people. The twisted metal of the station wagon on the freeway, all those years ago. Ayden. My dear Ayden. The pills could never dull my memory of him. I forced the images back down. I wasn't prepared to face the horror that I'd worked so hard to suppress. Not now. Maybe when I felt healthier in my body and soul. My psyche. It's a story for another time—you'll have to wait.

WE CROSSED THE BRIDGE that crouched over the mouth of the Cataract Gorge at around midday. A small boat meandered down the river, people waving and taking happy snaps on its deck, oblivious to our dubious band cruising into town like characters from a cheesy Spaghetti Western. The rocky slopes seemed sad to me, like they harbored secrets. Dark secrets. I was glad when we pulled up to our accommodation. Glad for a place to rest and drink and forget. Remember I said I was never a huge drinker? Well, I was willing to give it a red-hot go. The structure was Tudor-style and as I hopped out of the truck, I imagined I was in Europe. Maybe a small village in Austria. A bold fantasy, as I've never left Australia before, though the notion was appealing under the current circumstances.

We checked into our rooms and I threw myself onto my bed, the sound of Bronson scuttling about, exploring the place, fading into distant rhythm. I stared at the rafters in the ceiling for what could have been an hour; I wasn't entirely sure. A knock at the door made my heart skip a beat and I wandered over, peering through the window cautiously and pulling up the leg of my jeans, my fingers grazing my knife's butt. It was Beefa. I undid the latch and bid him entry.

"Let's hit the pub, Z. Try some of the local cider," said Beef.

"That's a great idea," I replied. "You guard my stuff!" I said to Bronson. He didn't look amused. "And no barking. You're not meant to be in here."

The drinking hole attached to the hotel was decked out like an inn from the time of Henry the Eighth. White walls encased thick wooden beams that looked roughly hewn from trees that once grew in an old growth forest. The portly publican exchanged our drink orders with amiable patter and soon we were imbibing the sweet flavor of Tasmanian apples. The booze went straight to my head and I found myself pitching a game to Beefa—one where we'd liken each punter in the place to a particular animal. Beef wasn't convinced.

"That guy, the one in the newspaper boy cap, with the long bushranger beard," I began.

Beefa pretended to stretch so he could get a good look. "Okay. Go on. You're going to do this no matter what, aren't you?"

"You know I am," I replied. "Anyway, the ginger-bearded fellow over near the window. He's like a hipster ferret."

"A ferret?" Beefa hazarded another glance. "Actually, yeah. I can see that," he added, with an uncharacteristic chuckle in his voice.

"Now, you do one!" I enthused.

"Fine." Beefa looked left and right before locking onto a target. "That lady. The one with the pointy nose. Some kind of bird?"

"Now here's where we need to lay down some ground rules. You gotta' be specific."

"You want a species?" Beef clarified.

"Yes!"

"A ... heron," said Beefa confidently.

"A heron?" I repeated. "Well done. The student has already become the master."

The hipster ferret stood up suddenly and I feared we'd been made. When he ambled over to our table, I felt a sinking feeling in my belly. Could he have really heard me from way over on the far side of the pub?

"Good evening," said the ferret.

"Hello," I offered awkwardly.

"Mate," was all Beefa said before taking a slug from his bottle.

"Are you new in town?" asked Ferret-Face.

"Just visiting," I said. Had he mistaken my game for interest?

"Are you two ... together, or..." Ferret's voice trailed off.

"Yes!" I blurted. Beefa's eyes met mine and I tried to apologize with my eyebrows.

"Oh," Ferret looked dejected. "Well, if you need anyone to show you around ... I run a little service, driving here and there," he said.

'A little vague,' I thought to myself. "Sounds great. We'll keep you in mind," is what I said.

"Here's my card," said Ferret, handing his details over. They were printed on clearly recycled cardboard. His logo was an apple in the shape of Tasmania with a little van working its way across its breadth. Bloody hipsters.

"Thanks heaps," I replied. Thanks heaps? Who still says that?

As Ferret exited the pub, I looked over his card. "Ty Fiddler," I read out to Beefa.

"What is that? Some sort of South East Asian fish?" quipped Beef.

"Look at you, gradually mastering the art of comedy," I shot back. "No, it's Ferret's name. He runs the Traverse Tassie Tour service. Not sure I'd want to hop in a van driven by some guy named Fiddler," I said before finishing my drink.

"Copy that," said Beefa. "Time for some friendly fire?"

That means 'let's drink some shots' in Beef-ese, just so you know. "You read my mind," I replied.

BRONSON SLURPED THROUGH the remnants of the takeaway curry I didn't remember buying. It may as well have been a bulldozer shoveling granite as far as my throbbing head was concerned. I sat up too quick and a tiny tsunami in my stomach had me bolting for the toilet. I dry retched a little, but gratefully, failed to follow through. The echo of an uncertain quantity of hard liquor haunted my mouth and nose and I crawled back under the covers, still in my clothes from the night before. That's when Beefa chose to make an entrance; the prick sounded more chipper than I would have liked.

"First of all: you failed to lock your door," he rebuked.

"Do you have coffee?" I mumbled from under the doona.

"No," he replied flatly.

"Then you shall not pass!"

"You need to come and see this," he added. I knew he wouldn't take no for an answer. "I spotted it on my morning jog."

"You went jogging?"

"Come on," he urged.

After kidding myself that I could splash my face with cold water and wash away the feeling that someone had taken a dump in my skull, I followed Beefa outside. The sun had barely made an appearance and I cursed the man under my toxic breath. We tramped out past the carpark, along the wall of the front office and down the sidewalk until we reached a small path that seemed to lead nowhere. After hauling my still-drunk ass after Beef for what felt like ages, we came to a scene that my eyes had trouble taking in.

I stared at the thing for a while but my brain wouldn't acknowledge what it was. Beefa crouched down next to the curiosity and then gestured to a spot a little way further down. There amongst thick bracken and overhanging bush was a sight I'll never forget. The object just near my feet was a severed human hand. Arranged under the foliage were an arm. A leg. Entrails. And worst of all: a familiar head. The face sported a ginger beard and looked mildly ferret-like.

What kind of hell had we escaped to?

Don't miss out!

Visit the website below and you can sign up to receive emails whenever Kira Parke publishes a new book. There's no charge and no obligation.

https://books2read.com/r/B-A-KFEH-EFYIB

BOOKS 2 READ

Connecting independent readers to independent writers.

Also by Kira Parke

Tropic Storm
Protected
Cyclone

Standalone
The Goddess of the Sea
They Never Came Back
Envious Green